Jean Christie

MISS GIARDINO

MISS GIARDINO

a novel by
Dorothy Bryant

Ata Books
Berkeley, California

Some of the places in this book are real,
but the characters and incidents are fictitious.

Library of Congress Catalog Number: 78-542-80
ISBN: 0-931688-01-9

Dedicated to my parents
Giuditta Chiarle Calvetti
and
Joseph Calvetti
who also survived a long journey

MONDAY

SHE WAS LYING on her back. In a bed. Not her bed. She breathed the odor of boiled, disinfected sheets. Her arms lay at her sides, straight, as if placed, arranged, outside the sheets. She lay like a dead body, arranged. But she couldn't be dead. She could hear voices.

"I didn't find any injury." Woman's voice. "Scraped elbow. Otherwise no superficial signs of fracture or internal bleeding. Bump on the head...doesn't look bad enough to...we'll run tests, of course." A doctor?

"Could she have had a heart attack or something?" Man's voice. "If I could have something a little more definite for my report..."

"I doubt it. Pulse a little rapid. Her color's good even though she was quite chilled. I think she's coming around."

"Okay if I ask her some questions?"

"Go ahead."

"Mrs. . . . Miss Gardino?"

"Giardino," she corrected automatically, "like jar." She opened her eyes. They stood together on the right side, the woman in white, the man in dark blue. Their faces were a blur. "My glasses."

"I put them in her purse," said the man. "They'd been knocked off." He reached behind, then swung forward a pouchy black bag, putting it on the bed next to her right hand. She looked at it. Was that her purse? "Want me to...?" He opened the bag, reached in, and brought out her glasses.

"Thank you." She put them on, curling the thin metal around her ears in a familiar, comforting movement. Faces cleared. She saw a broad-faced Latin woman in a white coat, stethoscope sticking out of the pocket; a pale, chunky man with thick sideburns, very young. He held a pad and pencil and wore a gun. Policeman. "What happened to me?"

"That's what I was going to ask you," said the young policeman. "A garbage collector found you."

"Where?"

"In front of Camino High School. Call came in at four a.m." He looked at his tablet. "Lying on your side. One shoe off, coat torn, purse ten feet away. Would you mind looking in your purse to see if anything is missing?"

She poked into the open bag, pulling out a wallet, checkbook, comb, handkerchief, toothbrush, pen, notebook.

"Is it all there? Your money?"

"I...I don't know. I..." A lost feeling crept over her like a chill. She didn't know whether anything was missing. She didn't know what should be there. Everything she touched seemed vaguely familiar, but...

"It looks like someone attacked you. Is that what happened? Could you give a description..."

The woman in white put up one hand in a gesture that silenced him. "What can you remember?"

She frowned and closed her eyes, then opened them again. She could not describe the blank in her mind. She shook her head.

"What about your name? You know your name."

She thought. "Giardino. You said it. How did you know my name?"

"It was on the library card in your wallet," said the policeman. "Your address too. 22 Phoenix Street. That ring a bell?"

"What's your first name?" asked the doctor.

She waited, but nothing came. She blinked, then looked from the woman to the man, as if she could search out the name by watching their faces.

The doctor picked up the wallet and glanced at something. "Is it Mary, or Emily, or Anna, or..."

"Anna. That's it. Anna Giardino. I couldn't remember for a moment. But when you said it, I knew. Have I had a stroke or something? I can't remember. Amnesia? But I haven't lost my memory. It's just that...I need to be reminded."

The doctor was nodding. "You've had a shock. A fall. You don't remember anyone accosting you?"

She shook her head.

The doctor shrugged. "It's not unusual to lose your memory this way. It's only temporary. Tomorrow you'll remember." She gave Anna a soft, reassuring smile, but her eyes remained sharp and

2

professional, watching Anna's eyes.

"I don't have amnesia."

"That word doesn't mean anything. You'll remember. Then you'll be able to tell the police what happened."

"Yes." She closed her eyes again.

"That's it. Just rest and let your mind wander. Free associate."

"That's what they all do," she said sharply. "Then they write it all down and call it an essay."

"Who?"

"My..." She opened her eyes. "Yes, my students. I'm a teacher. No. No, I'm not...not anymore." Her eyes closed. "I'm very tired. I want to sleep."

"She should rest now."

"Well," said the policeman, "if you say she didn't have a heart attack or anything, I'm going to write it up as another probable attack by unknown assailant. In that neighborhood, that's probably it." His voice drifted away, dropped lower, but Anna could still hear. "Crazy old woman, to walk around that part of town in the middle of the night. Wonder she didn't get killed."

They were out in the hall now, but before the door wheezed shut, Anna heard the woman's voice again. "If that's what happened, she may never remember the attack itself. Often they don't, especially if they were badly frightened. If she does remember, I'll tell her to call you."

Alone now, Anna opened her eyes. A faint gray light came from the window, too faint for her to be sure whether it was dawn or just the glow from street lights. But the noises from the corridors outside the room were getting louder. It must be dawn, the early, dark beginning of the hospital day, that busy last round of medications and thermometers before the end of the night shift. She felt herself in a soothing neutral place, comfortingly familiar because all hospital rooms are the same. Crowded yet empty. Anonymous, yet instantly identifiable as what they were. *Hospital. Mama in the hospital again. She is really dying this time. Quiet and patient, of course, always quiet and patient. Her old sunken face grows young as she nears the end, soft and pink, wrinkles and lines erasing. Eyes the same as always, wide, blue, innocent, accepting, always accepting her powerlessness.*

Does she pray? No, her lifelong praying has stopped. She is beyond prayers.

She sees a vision. Each time she looks toward the window she sees,

3

not the dingy building across the street, but something that makes her wide eyes shine. She describes it to me: a broad, blue river, streaming out to the horizon, flowing beyond sight, wide and deep. Above the streaming water, light falls from the sky, bright, warm showers of color and light, falling.

"You see it?"

"No, Mama."

"All colors. Like angel wings." A confused, uncertain look comes over her face. She listens to her own words and does not know what they mean. "Like angel wings?" She smiles. "I make no sense."

Then she is back in her past again. She tells me again the old story, how she journeyed from the village at the top of the Italian boot, across the ocean, with her three children. How she cried when she left her family, her friends, knowing she would never see them again. But she had to go. Her place was with her husband, already six years in the United States. He had saved the money now, and she must go to him. Alone and afraid. Seasick. Through all the days of the voyage she lay as if dead, her children huddled around her. "You remember, Anna?"

I shake my head. "I wasn't born yet, Mama."

She shakes her head and smiles at her mistake. "No, no, you were born here. That is right." She closes her eyes, but she is not asleep. Only resting.

In a moment she opens them again to tell me about the land I never saw. The Old Country, fixed forever in radiant panorama. How green the foothill meadows, how sweet the oranges, how golden the sunrise as they walk to the factories set in the fields of her grandfathers. And Michello, her handsome Michello, who sings like an angel and plays all musical instruments and reads books and chooses her above all the girls in the village. "Your papa, how he loved me!"

Then again she turns her head toward the window to see the bright vision: the streaming river, the rain of light. "You see it?"

"No, Mama."

"All colors. Like angel wings."

"Ah, good, you're awake." A stout nurse with red hair stood over Anna. "Supposed to take your blood pressure again before I go off." She wrapped Anna's arm and began pumping. "How are you feeling?"

"Is this Saint Paul's Hospital?" Anna asked.

"That's right. You're that accident case, aren't you?"

4

"My mother died in this hospital. Eight years ago. She was almost ninety."

The nurse nodded indifferently as she read the gauge, then unwrapped Anna's arm. She did not realize Anna's accomplishment: catching, pinning down, placing a memory.

After she left, Anna turned to look toward the window again. Perhaps I am dying, she thought, and, like Mama, will see a vision. "Nonsense," she muttered aloud. She would see no visions, being neither patient, nor saintly, nor believing. And she was not dying, only lying here, wondering what had happened, watching the window as if the light rising outside it would gradually reveal her past, her life, herself. *Window. Stay by the window and watch for Papa. Look down the muddy road, up the hill, to where he comes from the mine. I must watch, must see him come over the hill, tall and pale under the coal dust, dark, with an angry face, angry even when it smiles. I wish he would never come. Watch. Soon as I see him, I must run, run up the road to meet him, take his lunch pail and carry it home. If I don't watch, if I read or daydream, he will come crashing and shouting into the cabin. "No one meets me? No one cares if I come home? I should just send the money to feed all of you? I might as well stay in the mine?" He will shout until he starts to cough. He will cough until his face turns white and his black eyes dart around the cabin, like the rat Mike caught last week, eyes looking for some way out, some little slit to slip through and escape its death.*

Mama says I look like Papa. Tall and thin like him, with his black hair and black eyes. I wish I didn't. The others, Mike and Alfonsina and Victorina, all look like Mama. Golden hair and wide blue eyes and small bodies that go soft when there is enough to eat. There never is. Enough for Papa to drink, Mike says. That bad smell Papa has sometimes when he comes home, that bad smell means he will shout and fight with Mike, and Mike will run out. Papa says he works so we can eat. But he leaves the money in the saloon, Mike says. Mama washes for miners who are alone, whose families are still in the Old Country. She hides the money under the olive oil can. "Don't tell Papa." When the food is gone, Mama takes some coins from under the can, enough for another sack of polenta.

The others say, "Mama, let's go back home." They tell me about home, but I don't believe them. Home is, the world is, a cabin on a muddy road up the hill to a mine. It is called Illinois, Colorado, Utah, Montana. We move, but it is always the same cabin, road, mine. We move west, going to California, always going to California. But it stays the same, always the cold, the pot of polenta to stir on the stove, the muddy road between the cabins, the men on the road, walking, coughing. I know them all by their cough. There goes Mr. Santucci. I know without looking, by his cough.

"No sign of Papa?"

"No, Mama."

She sighs, and we do not look at each other. We know where he is.

I try not to think about him. I think about the other end of the road, down the hill, the long house where the thin lady rang the bell to open the school. She taught us all to write our names. I draw my name in great swirls over and over again. Everywhere, with my finger, in the mud outside our cabin, in the dust on the pipe of the wood stove, in the soap suds of Mama's tub of clothes, steaming, always steaming, on the frosted window while I wait for Papa. But the teacher has gone away. No more school till another thin lady comes. But I can read. Somehow I have learned to read. At first I only held, hugged, smelled the books, but now I can read them. I am the only one in the family who reads English. I hold the book the last teacher left with me, but I do not dare to read now. I must watch out the window. Watch for Papa.

Then it is dark, and Mama says not to wait anymore, come and eat.

I am in bed when he stumbles into the cabin. I wake up hearing the muttering, rumbling words, like the growling of the mine guard's dog. I crawl over Alfonsina, over Victorina, out of the bed, and I go to the doorway. Mama sits at the table, a blanket wrapped around her. Her eyes look sleepy but afraid. She stands up, offers Papa some food. He does not answer. She sits. He says she does not want to feed him. She gets up again, gets the plate of food she has kept for him. He pushes it away. "Cold, not fit to eat." He stands over her, over the table. He swells up with anger, and his swelling chokes me. I see the fight coming, the fury. Nothing can stop it. He wants it. He needs it.

Mama is already crying.

"Stupid woman, stupid!"

Now everyone is up. Mike puts on his clothes and goes out, slamming the door. He can do that, he is a boy, almost a man, already working in the mine. He can walk out, go to a friend, even go to the saloon. Alfonsina hugs Mama, they cry together. Victorina yells, "Leave Mama alone! You're drunk again!" She grabs the heavy iron that always sits on the stove waiting to be heated and then pushed *across the wash Mama does for the miners. "If you touch Mama, I'll kill you!"*

Papa chases Victorina around the kitchen table. She dodges him and laughs when he stumbles and gasps. He cannot move fast without gasping and losing his breath. He grabs a knife from the sink and throws it at her. She ducks. The knife sticks in the wall behind her. Alfonsina and Mama wail. Victorina screams. Papa stands leaning on the cold stove, shaking his fist, at Victorina, then at God, looking up at the ceiling.

I stand in the bedroom doorway, watching. He turns to me, stops and looks at me. His black eyes look into my black eyes. I don't let him see I am afraid. I show him nothing but fierce black eyes like his. I don't believe what Mama and the others say about the Old Country, about how he sang and was happy. I don't believe in that man. I only know this one, this cruel, mean man who sleeps in our cabin, this monster like the giants in the book of fairy tales the last teacher gave me.

"And you! What are you looking at!"

I say nothing.

"The hard one, eh? Hard and skinny, eh? You don't cry!" He almost smiles, to give me a small opening, so I can reach in to touch his anger, make it burst like the bubbles in Mama's wash tub. But I don't move. I make my eyes narrow and fierce, the way I have to do on the first day of new school in each new town, when I stand tall and pretend to be older and stronger than the bullies.

"Answer me!"

I say nothing.

"Won't talk? Talk! Answer me! I'll make you answer!" He comes at me. Mama and Alfonsina scream. Victorina steps between us, swinging the iron. He pushes her, and she crashes against the wall. I stand still, saying over and over in my head, I hate you, I hate you. I know if I stop saying it I will flinch, fall, even cry like Mama. I won't let him make me cry. I will die first.

He stops in front of me, stands over me, then starts to shake and cough. I do not move while he coughs, breathes great sucks of air, the way I did when I almost died of whooping cough. "Answer me, talk. I'll make you talk." But his voice is already softer. He stands with his hand over me, but does not hit me. His hand hangs in the air over my head. My head bends back as far as it can go, so that I can keep looking into his eyes as he looks down at me, coughs down at me. His

7

hand droops. He shakes his shoulders. "This one is too afraid to talk."

"I am not afraid," I say. Quietly. In English. Somehow I know the words in English will hit his eyes like a whip. He blinks. The new language, the language of the people outside the family, outside the cabin. The language of the people who own the mines. It is my language too. I alone in the family speak it without accent, read it, think in it.

I will never, never speak to him again but in English. I will save Italian for Mama. All my life, all her life, I will caress her with the easy, good-humored Piedmontese dialect, the tongue of golden sunsets and sweet oranges, of the place that is forever home to her. But to Papa I will speak only the language of this new country, my country, that promised him a new life but instead brings him to a new kind of death.

After a while he does the same, speaks to me only in broken English, laughing and saying, "You think I am a stupid immigrant, eh, but I speak English too." He stops calling me Anna. To him I am "the skinny one" or "the stick" or, more and more, "the American."

"Miss Guy-ar-dinna!"

Anna opened her eyes. "It's a soft G, and the i is pronounced like ee. Jar-deeno. Giardino. It means garden."

"Well, nothing wrong with you, knock on the head or not." A plump, black face smiled patronizingly at her, the typical nursing smile. "Want to be raised up?"

"Yes, please."

The nurse pressed a button which, with a whirring sound, brought Anna upward so that she could look more directly into the dark face. She felt stirrings of uneasiness, as if the nurse's face disturbed a sleeping shadow of memory which turned over and then lay still again.

"Doctor says he wants some forms filled out if you can remember." She offered some pieces of paper, then left the room. Anna filled in a few of the blanks. She was able to manage occupation and next-of-kin; that would be Victorina. The nurse came back, set down a tray of food, and looked at the papers. "Well, you haven't forgotten too much."

"I can't remember what happened yesterday, but things from fifty years back are clear as if I'm living them now."

The nurse nodded and smiled indulgently, as if to say old people were like that, living in the past, selecting happy memories to live, instead of facing present problems. "Might as well enjoy it."

8

Anna started to say that her early memories were far from enjoyable, but one glance at the nurse's face changed her mind. Anna hoped she had never treated her mother that way, looked at her that way. She was sure she hadn't, not even in those last feeble years, not even at the end when Mama saw visions of the heaven she had surely earned.

After the nurse left, Anna ate a little. Then, turning one way and another she found the set of buttons on a small disk hanging from the bed. Experimenting, she found the one which lowered the bed. The sun streamed in through the window. But now she was very sleepy. Memories stood in line, ready to crowd in on her, but she closed herself, held them off.

She slept. Most of the time she dozed lightly, half aware of the bustle of the hospital around her. But occasionally she dropped deeper into sleep, and whenever she did, she found herself watching a fire. She stood in front of it, a great fire. It burned and burned, but she could not tell what was burning. She rose to half-awake dozing, then fell back into fire-watching sleep. Each time she half-woke she asked herself, what's burning? She could see nothing but flames.

Then came a roar, a deep, underground explosion. A series of buried explosions rumbled, shaking the whole world. Her eyes snapped open, her body jolted awake. *Mike! Oh, Jesus, Marymotherofgod, Mike is down there.*

Only a few months, Mama said, Mike will work in the mine only a few months before we will have enough to go to California, a ranch and a few chickens, maybe a cow, a warm place like the Old Country, but rich. The few months stretch on to a year, two years, and Mama tells me over and over, soon, a few months. I listen as I do to the fairy tales she tells, and I believe her no more than I believe her version of Tom Thumb who, eaten by a cow, comes out alive in a pile of manure.

And now Mike is dead, killed in the explosion.

Papa comes home and sits. He does not say Mike's name. He says nothing at all. He sits. He does not drink. For three days he sits. There is no wake, no funeral. Mike and the others lie under the tons of dirt. The mine is a cemetery for Mike.

After three days Papa goes back to the mine, to a special mine where the men earn more money because the fumes and dust are worse. Three years in that mine, the lady next door tells Mama, are enough to kill a man. Papa works there six months. We sell everything. We eat polenta alone. And Papa does not drink. At the end of

9

six months we have train fare to California.

The fairy tales were true! We reach California in late summer. We pick fruit in the Gilroy orchards. We live in a cabin like all the cabins we have lived in before. But this cabin is in the orchard, where we can eat all we want: peaches, apricots, prunes. We all pick fruit and give our money to Mama. Papa does not drink. When he calls me the American, he almost smiles. But mostly he says nothing. He is too tired after the day's work to do anything but squat, leaning against the post outside the cabin door, watching the sun go down.

In the fall, everyone works in the cannery, all but me. I am too young. I wander through the warm, dry orchards, kicking up the powdery dirt with my toes.

One day I walk into town and discover the public library. A tiny room behind the barber shop. A few shelves. Sets of classics bound in something like leather. They smell moldy. Ladies' novels. Boys' adventures. Lots of religious books. A white haired lady opens the library every day from one to four. She is pale and dry, with sharp, neat edges to her body and her words. She looks at me, then tells me to wash my hands before I touch the books. She asks if I am one of the eye-talians working in the fields. "Then you can't take books out, you'll just lose them or move on without returning them."

But every day she finds me waiting outside when she comes to open the library, then has to send me home when she closes it. Her face softens, almost smiles, and she gives me a little white card. Now every day I carry home a book, then bring it back to exchange for another the next day. By the time I have finished the thirteen volume set of Mark Twain, the sharp, neat lady is asking me why I am not in school.

She walks home with me to the cabin and tells Mama and Papa about the law. Mama and Papa sit frozen by the words of this sharp-edged lady. After she leaves, Papa says, "Let her go to school, she's no good for anything else. The law, the law. She must not work in the cannery, she must go to school. What for? She can read and write already. She reads too much. The law... it makes her useless and self-ish. She is selfish enough, the American. She thinks she is better than her family." But I can see that he is afraid of the librarian, and afraid of the law.

The next year a small ranch goes up for sale by a paisano, an immigrant like us. He asks how much money we have saved, then says it is enough for a downpayment. I read the contracts with Papa, I

10

translate the hard parts, but I do not understand. Does Papa under-
stand? He signs the papers, Mama signs the papers, and she kisses me,
she kisses everyone, and laughs and cries. The dream has come true.

But it is only a dream. What do we know about prunes? Even in the
old country Mama and Papa worked in factories, keeping only tiny
bits of land the grandfathers had farmed, growing nothing but
vegetables for the table, a few herbs. The prune trees catch a blight.
The chickens die of some mysterious disease. And Papa's breathing
shortens to gasps between coughs, more coughs. It is too late for the
sunshine and fresh air to cure him. The disease in his lungs grows
more slowly, but it grows. He is not fit for the long hours of heavy
outdoor work. And he knows nothing of prunes and blights, of
mortgages and markets, of water rights and big land owners.

But I go to school every day for a full year, the first full year of
school in my life. I come home to a ranch house bigger than the cabins
we lived in before, and warmer. But it is a haunted house.

All that winter the house is haunted by a steady tapping, a soft,
sharp knocking. I open the door, but no one is ever there. The
knocking comes at night, in the early morning, any time. We listen to
it, and after a while, we do not look at each other when it starts. All of
Mama's fears from the Old Country are revived. She hangs charms
against evil spirits all around the house, mixing Madonnas with ugly
dolls made of bits of mud, string, chicken feathers and hair. Papa
goes around tearing them down, cursing her ignorance, but when the
knocking starts again, he is silent, except to mutter curses against the
man who sold him a sick ranch with a huge mortgage. His mutterings
grow to hoarse shouts, then die away as he leans against the sink,
breathing hard, trying not to cough. Then the tapping starts again,
like the knocking of final failure, defeat, knocking, knocking to be let
in to stay.

We lose everything, savings and ranch, everything but the clothes
we wear. The man from the bank that takes the ranch gives us the fare
to San Francisco. On the day we leave, we find the ghost, the
mysterious knocker: a woodpecker under the low, slanting roof.
Alfonsina laughs, but Papa throws a rock at it. His aim is good. The
bird falls. It dies slowly, its breast heaving. Alfonsina cries, then turns
away and runs. I watch her. Mama calls. But she keeps running and
never looks back. She marries a boy from the cannery. She never
writes to us. Two years later she dies in childbirth.

In San Francisco we move in with a cousin who lives in an old flat in

11

North Beach. Right away Papa quarrels with him because he talks about going back to Italy. Mama is silent while Papa attacks the Old Country and "the stupid, lazy idiots" who stay there or have no guts to work and fight instead of going back after a few years in America. Mama tells me most of the men who came when Papa came have gone back. What keeps him here? His pride? In Washington Square he meets friends of friends from the Old Country. He quarrels with all of them. "San Francisco is a cold city, full of fog like London, full of cold people like the English." The fog makes his cough worse. Mama says a woman told her the weather is better in the south-eastern part of the city, in the Mission District. There the fog backs up behind Twin Peaks, and the sun shines all day. There some factories and breweries are hiring.

We find two rooms over a store on Bartlett Street, just off Mission Street, a wide, store-lined street running clear through the city from the bay to the cemeteries, crackling with sparks shot off night and day from trolley cars. We have a kitchen, bath and bedroom. Victorina and I sleep on a couch in the kitchen beside a round oak table with four spindley, cane-bottom chairs. The wood stove is usually empty and cold, and we wear sweaters, because wood is too expensive to buy in the city. But we have a flush toilet.

And I have a miracle. Across the street a building is just being finished, a palace with columns and marble steps. And this marble palace is a public library, with a special entrance leading to a special room for children, including Italians. The librarian tells me that when I have read all the books in the children's room, she will give me a card which will admit me to the great marble staircase of the adult library. She watches me for a few weeks, then puts a thick, closely printed book in front of my face and commands me to read aloud to her. I do, and she gives me the card.

I climb the marble staircase to face another librarian, who sniffs, "How old are you?"

But I am getting used to these sharp, pale ladies. "Twelve," I whisper bravely, pushing my card at her to show that I am worthy to enter this quiet hall with its sacred smell of old bookbindings and glue, a smell that gives me the sense of peace and safety that Mama gets from the candles and incense of the church two blocks away. Now I leave our rooms during Papa's rages, running across the street to the palace of quiet and reason, calming my shaking hands by holding a book in them.

12

For the rages have started again, even without liquor. He is too sick now to drink at all. Not even a glass of wine. A few steps across the room tire him, and his hands shake all the time. He goes to the county hospital, but the doctors can do nothing for him. He might live for years, they tell him, but will only, slowly, get worse. They give him cigarettes, the first he has ever touched. White, hard-tipped cylinders. He is to smoke one every morning.

A new ritual begins. He gets up every morning and goes to the bathroom where he stands over the toilet. Inhaling on the cigarette, he coughs, spits, then gives a long, shouting moan which he says helps to clear his air passages. His voice grows stronger, his moans become loud shouts heard in the grocery store below. The storekeeper complains. The rooms are full of the acrid smoke when I wake every morning, a strange smoke I cannot name until I breathe it again, forty years later, in the girls' rest room at Camino High School, during my last teaching years: marijuana.

Mama and Victorina find work in the cork factory on Potrero Avenue. I start to work with them, but someone tells my age. Again there are visits to our rooms, this time by a more frightening, official looking man. I must go to school. So I am sent running down Mission Street every morning to a building only slightly less blessed than the public library. I listen amazed when the other children say they hate school and call the teachers mean and strict. Compared to Papa, they are saints, easy to placate, even easy to please.

Victorina disappears on her eighteenth birthday. She has run off with a boy she met in the cork factory. Now I am the only one left. "A useless mouth to feed, her nose in a book all day." Mama works all day in the factory. Papa sits in the window, silently looking out, always there waiting when I come home from school, watching me when I do the cleaning and cooking. He has stopped speaking to Mama. He saves all his anger for me, starting as soon as I get home: I take too long getting home; I put his medicine in the wrong place; I put too much salt in the soup. Once, when he gets sick, he accuses me of poisoning his food. I deny it, in English. He raises his hand, but cannot get across even that tiny room to hit me. He leaves his fist in the air, calling on God to witness the curse of his child, the American, thriving in the air that strangles him. Then he curses God.

I find an ad in the paper: mother's helper live in room and board small salary for girl 22 Phoenix Street. The house is only a few blocks away, up the hill. I climb up to Phoenix Street and find the tall

13

victorian house owned by a shopkeeper on Mission Street. "Jews!"
says Papa, but he says I can go if I give him all I earn. "Go. Work.
Make yourself useful for a change."

"Miss Giardino?"

Anna opened her eyes. It was a different nurse this time, a pale, empty-eyed girl, pregnant and very tired-looking.

"You have a visitor."

Anna looked at the old woman who stood by the side of the bed. She was fat and fierce looking, as if puffed up with anger. Her hair was dyed reddish brown and her face was covered by a mask of make-up. Red lipstick ran into the wrinkles radiating outward from her lips. She wore a heavy brown coat and a matching hat, very expensive looking, very heavy and ugly.

"Do you know me?"

"Victorina."

"They said you couldn't remember anything."

"I remember some things. I was just thinking of you, in fact. Did you come all the way from San Jose?"

"Where else would I come from? Yes, from San Jose. They called me, said you were in an accident. You look all right."

"I'm fine."

"What happened?"

"I don't remember that yet." She felt an uneasy quiver, her first stab of fear, and she wondered how and why she should fear what she could not remember.

Victorina pulled a chair to the side of the bed and sat down. "I just got back from Reno. My feet are killing me."

Anna could not think what she could say to her sister. They saw each other at most once or twice a year since their mother died. Victorina's husband had died at the same time. She had fought with him for nearly fifty years, as if continuing the fight with her father. When he died, she was lost. She turned to religion, not the Catholic Church of her childhood but a small cult devoted to development of occult powers and something called "mind raising." It turned out to be not so sinister as it sounded to Anna. The most important thing it had brought to Victorina was an introduction to a friend, a slot machine addict who was also a medium. When not engaged in seances, Victorina spent her time in Reno, standing for hours before a slot machine, wearing her pink house slippers, her "lucky" slippers, and sipping gin and juice. She was seventy-five years old.

14

"I'm sorry they bothered you," said Anna. "There's nothing for you to do, no reason to have driven that far."

"I don't mind coming," Victorina said irritably. "You're just lucky you weren't killed. Why you stayed on in that neighborhood all these years I'll never know. Full of those Mexicans and Blacks and... perverts! You should..."

"It's a very nice neighborhood and I like it," snapped Anna.

"It's not safe!" Victorina persisted. "Things have changed. It's not the same like when we were girls. You don't have to live there, you could live in one of those nice apartments out of town, San Jose, Walnut Creek, Marin, any of those nice complexes. You can afford it, you..." Her voice trailed off. She seemed to know that Anna would not listen, would not argue with her.

"I've thought of many old things today," said Anna, looking off into space. "I've been remembering things."

"Remembering things? What things?"

"I started with thinking about Mama, in the hospital, at the end. You know she saw visions?"

"It was the drugs they gave her. Made her see things. She was getting senile anyway."

"She was not! She forgot things, but she was quite rational to the very end." Another argument starting. Anna sighed. It should be possible to talk with Victorina without arguing. "I lived with her, after all," Anna insisted more quietly, "up to the last few weeks in the hospital. She was just the same as always..."

"Afraid, superstitious, weak..."

Anna shook her head. "Sometimes I think you hated her more than you did Papa. I don't understand."

"Easy. Easy to understand. Do you think I ever let my husband lay a hand on my children? Do you think I would put up with any of that? Of course, we had our differences." Anna smiled at the thought of Victorina's long battle with her husband. Even when he was dying, she nagged him, accused him of not trying to stay alive. "But I would never let him treat the children the way Papa did us."

"What could she do?"

"Walk out! I'd have scrubbed floors on my hands and knees to raise my children, but I'd have left that man."

"So would I," said Anna, suspecting that she would have left while Victorina would have stayed and fought. "But Mama wasn't like us. She couldn't. It wasn't possible for her even to think of leaving her

15

husband. Surely you can forgive her for that. I got the worst of all from Papa, and I don't blame her."

"You got the worst? You were always the favorite. You were the smart one, you went to college. What do you think he said to me every time I saw him, why aren't you smart like your sister?"

"He did? Yes, he would. He knew how to be cruel. Do you realize he was only fifty-three when he died? We've lived so much longer than he did. I'm old enough to be his mother."

"And just like him."

Anna nodded. "The older I get, the more I look like him."

Victorina shook her head. "I mean inside. I don't know what it is. Something driving you. It makes you not need people, makes you do things, like going to college, to make a place for yourself above us, above..."

"You still see it that way!"

"Yes, why not say it. Better than others. I still remember his funeral. You, coming back from the university, just graduated, everyone so impressed, talking about you, not about him, talking to you, asking what you were going to do now, the college graduate."

"They were just being polite. They were Mama's friends, not his. They couldn't say a good word for him, so they showed interest in his children."

"Hypocrites. There must have been nearly a hundred people there, none of them who'd speak a word to him if he was alive..."

"All there for Mama's sake, and for ours."

"For ours? What did we care? I was glad he was dead. I wasn't a hypocrite, like you."

"Like me? What do you mean? I was as glad as you. I never tried to hide it. Even if he'd been good to us, with his sickness he was better off dead."

"Then what was that scene all about, that great act when you came in?"

"What act?"

"After the funeral, when we all came home. And those people came to my house, you know the way people used to do, we had them come to my house because you couldn't have them all in those crummy rooms over the store. And it was like a reunion, *paisani* who hadn't seen each other for years, been afraid to visit Mama for years, and everybody more relieved than anything else, relieved it was finally over and he was dead." She moved to the window, staring out on the

16

noisy, smoky street with hard eyes, hard voice, not looking at Anna anymore, not even really talking to her anymore. "And you were listening to old man Rossi, the only one who had a good word to say for him, talking about the Old Country and what a fine, intelligent, handsome boy Papa was in the Old Country, how everyone in the village said he'd go far. And then you were crying, and everyone said what a devoted daughter you were, and so smart too. When all the time, I knew you hated him more than I did, but you had to put on this little act for the crowd. I always respected you before that, but. . . when you did that. . ." Her voice dropped to a grating whisper as she muttered to the window, "You had to have that pose, the dutiful daughter who stayed after Alfonsina and I ran off and married and left Mama. But not you. Not perfect little Anna, who stayed by the deathbed and. . ." *I sit beside his bed, awkward, uneasy, though there is now nothing to be uneasy about, nothing to fear from him. No more rages, no more threats. Little breath in him now, no more than a few whispered phrases between long gasps. He whispers short, carefully chosen English phrases. What makes me uneasy is the strangeness of him. He is not the man I know, not Papa. Without his anger, his fury, his cruelty, what is left? A pale, thin man with thick black hair, gasping for air he cannot use, lying there, his thin, yellowish arms limp on the sheets. An uncertain man, opening his eyes from time to time to make sure I am here. Then, quieted by the sight of me, giving a slight nod and closing his eyes. His face is unlined, gaunt, the ascetic face of a saint. Where is the man I hate?*

For a week I have been sitting here, since he could not get out of bed, since the doctor refused to come and only sent more drugs, since Mama called and said he wanted me, only me. During my four years at the university he has refused to see me. The deserter, the American, dead to him. "You won't see me alive again," he had told me when I left.

But now, at the end, he wants me, only me. I must stay beside him so that when he opens his eyes he sees me. If I move from the rocking chair, he calls, gasping, "Anna," the name he has hardly ever spoken.

"I'm right here, Papa." During the day I sit in the old rocker. At night I lie on the floor on an old quilt. Mama sleeps on the couch in the kitchen.

On the fifth day his breathing grows more quiet. At first it seems smoother, easier. No more gasps. But there are long intervals between the shallow breaths. Longer. His skin turns ivory. His fingers twitch.

17

He opens his eyes, looks at me and whispers, "Ecco," as if summing up everything, as if looking at me and telling me that I am all he has to show for his life, his struggle. He closes his eyes again, and does not open them for hours.

Later that day he speaks again. "The American," he whispers. But there is no sarcasm or bitterness in his voice. "Smart." His tone is even proud. He fixes his dark eyes on mine. "You know," he says, with just a shadow of the old cruel irony, "you...are like...me... or you could...never done it."

That night I stay in the rocking chair, dozing lightly, waking with a start when the interval between his breaths grows long. Soon his breathing is too faint to hear at all. I stay awake, watching the slight rise and fall of his narrow, bony chest. Sometimes there is no motion, only the twitch of his fingers to tell me he is still alive.

About three in the morning he opens his eyes and looks directly at me. He is alert, and his breath seems to come easily. He can speak without gaps between words for gulps of air. "How does it go, at the university?"

"Fine, Papa."

"You are now a Bachelor of Arts?"

"Yes, Papa."

"Bene. And now, what do you do?"

"I will get a teaching credential and become a high school teacher."

"What will you teach?"

"English."

"Ah." He nods and tries to smile. "You still read many books."

"Yes, Papa."

Now there is silence again, but he does not close his eyes. He seems to be summoning all his strength to do something or say something. Something very hard, almost impossible. What can it be? I watch and wonder what he must accomplish before he dies, what it is that he must tell me.

"You know..." He is back to short phrases again, barely whispered through his blue lips. "I...like you."

It is as close as he can get. He cannot say he loves me. Yet, it comes through, like a burst of light, that he does. He loves me. He has envied me and hated me, abused me, resented me. He has projected upon me all his bitterness and disappointment. And yet he does love me. He has always loved me. It is true. It is inescapable. It is terrible.

He watches me, waits for my response. I sit dumb...hearing,

18

watching, seeing what I have never seen before. My mind sees that here is a new situation, calling for a new response. But my feelings, so long frozen against him, cannot thaw out at once. I sit, stiff, stuck, unable to respond, unable to give him the words he begs for, the simple, "I love you, Papa." Never mind if it is true or not, never mind if it is impossible. I must say it. To hold back will be cruel, more cruel than anything he has ever done to me.

But the moment comes and goes too quickly. His eyes close. They do not open again.

"I guess," Anna said, "I cried because I didn't hate him anymore." But her sister turned from the window and gave her a blank look. She had obviously forgotten what she was saying and had merely been staring out the window, lost in her own memories. "How are the children?" asked Anna, falling back on her last resort for conversation with people of the married, family world. She was beginning to feel very tired again. Now she would be able to rest while her sister sat down by the bed again and recited her complaints.

Her son lived in Los Angeles. Her first granddaughter had married last year and was pregnant. The other two were in college. But no one ever wrote to her. They were only an hour away by plane, but invited her only once or twice a year, and then she didn't feel welcome. Her daughter-in-law didn't like her. Her daughter lived right in San Francisco and had just divorced her second husband. "I told her, at fifty-three she's not going to find another husband. I blame her for the way all her children turned out, all long-haired freaks, one living like a savage off in New Mexico, another raising an illegitimate child like she was proud of it. Oh, I never see her, we just fight. I told her, you're just getting old now, we're mother and daughter, but we're just two old women now.

"I'll be honest, Anna, I used to think you missed something not having children, but maybe you did the right thing. No matter what you do with your life, when you're old, you're old, and that's all there is to it. So what did I have children for? No one wants you anymore. It doesn't matter which way we went, we end up in the same place."

Anna did not know what to say. Her head was beginning to hurt.

"I'll stay here, take care of you when you get out of the hospital."

"I don't need taking care of. I'm all right."

"I can stay downstairs in Mama's old apartment. Give me the key. I'll go get things ready for you. I'll stay until you feel strong."

Anna said nothing.

"You don't want me."

"No." Because Anna felt tired her tone was more blunt than she intended.

Victorina got up. "Well, you always were honest, I'll say that. We never really were sisters to each other. I thought, now, before we die. There's a lot we could do together. You never really had any fun, always studying, taking care of Mama. We could go to Reno on the weekends. I belong to three clubs, where people our age go, dancing, parties, all the things you're too poor or too busy to do when you're young."

Anna smiled. Her sister's life seemed such an appalling bore, it made her tired to think about it. But, of course, by her sister's standards Anna was the one whose life had been a bore. "We're too different. Being old doesn't change that." Victorina reached for her purse, then leaned over Anna and kissed her cheek with a closed, hard mouth. "Thank you for coming," said Anna.

At the door, Victorina pulled out a gauzy yellow handkerchief and dabbed her dry eyes, trying to cry, taking one more quick look to see the effect on Anna. Anna watched coolly, yet amazed. It always amazed her to see counterfeit feelings displayed coercively. Instead of making her reach out to her sister, ask her to stay, this display immobilized her. It had no more reality than an image on a television screen. Was she cold, unfeeling? She had been accused of coldness often enough. *"Oh, Miss Giardino, can't I have one more day to finish? I know I was late last time too, but I . . ."*

"But, Miss Giardino, I get A's in all my other classes. I never got a C on a paper before. My aunt used to teach English and she thought it was good!"

"Can't I make it up? No, I wouldn't call it cheating. Me, copy? No, I don't want to see your copy of the essay in the book. Oh, Miss Giardino, you can't flunk me and ruin my life!"

"Miss Giardino, you're so mean!"

"Miss Giardino, you a racist!"

The pale nurse came in again, this time with a lunch tray. Anna could not touch it. She felt too tired even to lift the tea bag out of the cup of hot water on the tray. She watched the water turning darker and darker, turning into an undrinkable, strong liquid, then cooling, cold.

When the nurse came back, she made a disapproving sound with her lips, shaking her head at the untouched food. Anna ignored her.

"Maybe your visitor tired you too much."

Anna nodded. It was true. She felt sleepy, sleepier than she had felt for a long time, for years, sleepier then she ever felt when going to bed at night. She began to yawn, one great yawn after another. She could not stop yawning.

The nurse watched her. "It's the shock. You're beginning to let go now. Just let go and sleep."

She was asleep before the nurse was out of the room. She slept through the afternoon, waking briefly to look at the tray they brought her, then falling asleep again. It was a deep, dreamless sleep broken occasionally by noises coming from the hall or by the loud, metallic crashes happening far away, far down the hospital corridor.

When night came she continued to sleep, but now she was dreaming again. She watched the fire again in her dream. But this time she could see what was burning. It was not the mine. It was Camino Real High School, the old school, burning fiercely behind its red brick facade, every window spouting red flames.

In her dream Anna was again the age she had been when the school actually burned down, shortly before she graduated, in 1922. She stood alone in front of it, in her dark, unfashionably long dress, her dark, unfashionably long hair hanging down her back. She watched the fire gutting the inside of the building while the red brick shell remained the same, solid, even unblackened by smoke.

"The fire is too hot to make smoke, the fire is all inside and the outer shell shows nothing."

She turned to see Mr. Simpson, the principal. He stood next to her, his rolled up plans for the new school sticking out of one pocket and his flute sticking out of the other. He often played his flute at school assemblies, and in his last year, after the new school was built, he walked through the halls playing it, like an old pagan priest conferring immunity from evil spirits.

"Then will you only rebuild the inside?" she asked, though she knew better.

"No, not possible, my dear, not possible. New wine in old bottles, you know. Come along, let's tear it down."

They moved closer to the tall building, looking at the flames through the long windows. There was no glass on the window openings, but she felt no heat from the flames.

"Cold fire, that's the worst kind," said Mr. Simpson.

He pointed at her and then at the brick wall, and she saw that he meant for her to tear it down, brick by brick. "Otherwise you see, my dear, we'll never get started building."

He raised his flute to his lips again and played while she stepped forward and pulled out a brick. She heard a crash behind the brick, as if something inside had collapsed. The flute music sounded higher, more piercing, as she pulled out another brick. One by one, brick after brick, she went on, pulling them out of the wall, listening to the crash within, throwing the bricks over her shoulder. She saw that no one would come to help her, though the streets were suddenly crowded with people who all looked familiar.

"I see no one else will lift a finger," she said loudly, but she was answered only by the continuing piping of the flute. She shrugged and went on pulling bricks, one by one, not counting, not thinking, resigned to her task.

TUESDAY

"WELL, YOU SLEPT all day and all night and woke up famous!" It was the black nurse again. Her face seemed more genuinely friendly than the day before. She was holding a newspaper in one hand. "I usually get the morning paper, read it just before I go off duty. This time I found you, right on page four."

She handed Anna the paper, which had been opened to page four and folded around the article. Then she picked up Anna's glasses from the table and gave them to her. While Anna read, the nurse moved around the room, opening window curtains, straightening the bed sheets, putting fresh water in the pitcher, and turning, after each task, to watch Anna's reaction to reading about herself.

CAMINO REAL TEACHER MYSTERY VICTIM

Former English teacher Miss A. Giardino, 68, was found yesterday morning at 4 a.m. unconscious on the sidewalk near Camino Real High School, apparently the victim of attempted robbery. Police said there were signs of violent attack, but that the contents of Miss Giardino's purse seemed intact, and theorized that when Miss Giardino resisted, the thief panicked and escaped without taking anything.

Dr. Consuelo Gans, who received the victim at St. Paul's Hospital, said that Miss Giardino had suffered shock and was unable to tell what had happened to her, but that her condition was good and she expected to release her after routine tests.

Miss Giardino resides at 22 Phoenix Street, overlooking Camino Park and Camino Real High School She attended old Camino Real High School (destroyed by fire in 1922) and taught at the new Camino Real from 1929 to 1969. When she retired, she was honored at a special dinner, as the only teacher in the city ever to put in such long service in a single school.

23

"Another toast to Miss. G. and her well-earned retirement!" And good riddance is what he's thinking. We never liked each other. Drunk. They're all drunk. When I think of the time I almost lost my job because someone saw me drinking a glass of wine in a restaurant with David! Times have certainly changed. But for the better?

A party for me? They hardly notice me. I sit here like a statue. That's how the young ones see me: a moldy monument. And the older ones? Just as much strangers as the young ones. Not a friend left. The few friends I had either died or left teaching long ago.

I get up and leave. No one notices. I won't be missed.

"That must be an old picture of you they used," said the nurse, coming back to the bed and leaning over Anna.

Anna recognized it. "It was taken during my first year of teaching."

"Well, it's still you, for sure."

"No, it isn't." Anna looked at the picture and shook her head. "It's another woman entirely."

The nurse refused to understand. "I think it's a very nice picture. Funny. . . how up to date it is."

"What do you mean?"

"Well, your hair's long, parted in the middle and rolled up there at the back of the neck. No make-up. Wire-rimmed glasses. Why, you look just like the young girls today. Funny how the styles change. What was in forty years ago comes back. Everything comes back if you just wait long enough."

Anna shook her head again. "I wasn't in fashion at the time. Women wore their hair short, shaved their eyebrows and penciled thin lines, wore layers of powder and rouge."

"Well, you were just ahead of your time."

Anna laughed. "Or behind. I was never sure."

"How do you feel today?"

"Fine. I want to go home."

"That's up to the doctor."

"I'm not her prisoner. I can go if I want to." Anna pulled back the covers and swung her legs over the edge of the bed. The nurse began to stammer something. Anna laughed again and said, "I'm just going to the bathroom."

Taking her purse, she went into the tiny room, urinated, then washed her face and brushed her teeth. She still had her own teeth, most of them, another inheritance from her father. As she looked in the mirror she thought of the newspaper picture. The face she saw in the mirror looked like the bone structure behind the smooth young face in the old photograph: sharp lines of nose and chin, skin dry and tight, as if all youthful smoothness had been eroded away. The hair was short now, but the glasses were still wire-rimmed. The eyes behind them were dark and intense as ever, though the surrounding skin had loosened and wrinkled. But there were no puffs or jowls as on the face of Victorina. Anna had stayed lean. The greatest change had come to her mouth. It seemed smaller, the lips thinner. Any movement creased lines all around it. The eyes might be the windows of the soul, Anna thought, but it was on and around the mouth that time, trouble and frustration made their marks.

Her breakfast tray was waiting when she came out. She was very hungry and ate everything on it.

She had just finished when a slender oriental man came in. He wore a white coat over a gold shirt with a broad, golden tie. "I'm Doctor Yogato. Neurology." He put out his hand, but when Anna grasped it, it felt limp. When she looked into his eyes, he looked down at his hand, which he was withdrawing slowly, letting it creep across the sheets. A reserved man, she thought, who's been told he should be friendly and shake hands with his patients, but who doesn't really feel it. "I hear you want to go home," he said, his eyes traveling all around the room as he spoke, and returning to her only when she looked away. He reminded her of so many of the oriental boys she had taught. They were never able, it seemed, to look a woman in the face.

"That's right," she said. "I'm feeling fine. I'd like to go."

He studied his fingernails. "Remember anything?"

Anna nodded. "Everything's coming back, starting with childhood memories I haven't thought of for years." She felt a little proud, like a student who has done her homework more thoroughly than the teacher expected.

Until he said, "What about. . .do you remember what happened to you?"

Then came the blank and the uneasy sense of danger unseen. She shook her head. "But I'm all right. I'd like to go home."

"I'd like to run a few tests on you first, just to be sure. At your age. . .x-rays, EKG. We've got a new brain-monitoring device I'd like to try on you. Just to check everything out before you go."

"How long will it take?"

"I'll order tests for this afternoon. We'll have the results right away. If everything is all right, you can go. Okay?"

"Okay."

As soon as the doctor left the room, the telephone rang. Anna looked at it for a moment, unable to believe that it had anything to do with her. Then she picked up the receiver. "Yes."

"Anna. My dear, I was just sitting here drinking my coffee and reading the paper, and there you were. Are you all right?"

"I'm fine, David. I'm perfectly all right. When did you get back?"

"Yesterday. I was thinking about calling you when. . . I'm still in jet shock, don't have the vaguest idea of time, and everything I look at has haloes around it or sparks flying off. I'm too old for traveling. This is my last trip."

Anna smiled. "You've been saying that for the past twenty years."

"Yes, but this time I mean it. I'm going to. . . but that can wait. Are you really quite all right?"

"They're going to take some tests to make sure, but, yes, I'm sure I'm all right."

"What's this about not remembering what happened?"

"I don't. But I'm going to, eventually. Yesterday I didn't even remember you."

"But you do now? Sure? Who am I?"

"David Stern. Man of a hundred talents. World traveler. Musician, actor, teacher."

"Exactly. You are quite well." He laughed. "What can I bring you?"

"Nothing, nothing at all. I'll be out of here tonight or tomorrow. Don't bother, don't take any trouble."

"Nonsense! I love to take trouble. See you in a little while."

He hung up before Anna could protest again. Of course, David loved to take trouble, loved doing things for people. There was a time, when he was in his late forties, clearly and finally a permanent bachelor, that there were a number of old ladies he constantly did things for. Now all his old ladies were dead, and Anna was the age that they had been, David only seven years younger. Anna thought, I am his last old lady. I suppose I was really his first old lady. She leaned back and smiled. Yes, at thirteen I was a very old lady indeed.

Mother's helper live in room and board small salary for girl 22 Phoenix Street. I hold the ad clenched in my fist and walk up the hill, two, three blocks, four. This is the first time I have climbed west from Mission Street, up and down steep little hills on the way up to Twin

Peaks. Everything changes, from little apartments over stores, like ours, to small houses, then higher up to a few big houses, spread out, with trees and terraced flower beds down the steep front to the street.

22 Phoenix Street is a house like that, with four others, at the top of the Phoenix Street hill, just where it dips down again, then tips up toward Twin Peaks. The house stands high up above the street. I climb the stone steps to the front garden, then another flight to the front porch. I twist the bell knob and hear a high jingling. While I wait, I turn around to look behind me and down.

Below, just a few blocks down, I can see the red brick building, Camino Real High School. How nice it would be, to be rich, to have the money to keep going to school, studying, doing nothing but learning all day. Some of the students at the high school even go on to college.

Down a few blocks more, yes, there's Mission Street. I can see the tall, gray library. Behind the library building is the store with our rooms up over it. I can't see that, but I know it's there. I know Papa is sitting in the window. I'm glad I can't see him. I look north, across all the rooftops. The sky is clear and I can see all the way to the Golden Gate. I even see little dots and puffs of smoke: ferry boats. One day I'll take Mama for a ride on a ferry boat and. . .

I hear the door open and turn around to see a small boy with thick, blonde curly hair, big blue eyes and pink, soft lips. He looks like one of the angels on the holy cards Mama brings home from church. He smiles. "I'm David, who are you?"

I open my fist and show him the ad.

"Oh, yes!" He grabs my hand and pulls me into the house. He runs through the hall to the back. "Mother, here's the girl to help you!" He turns to me. "What's your name?" Then he is pushing open the kitchen door. "Her name is Anna, isn't that a nice name!"

Mrs. Stern is short and dark, with a thick, round bosom. She looks surprised and confused, worried, as if she has just peeked out at the world from behind heavy curtains and is afraid of what she sees. David holds my hand tight and smiles and nods at his mother. She tilts her head, sighs, and nods with him as if she is used to giving him his way. I am hired without a word, and by the time she finds out I am only thirteen, it doesn't matter because she depends on me for so many things.

I move into the little basement room under the kitchen. There are only David and his parents in the big rooms above. The Sterns are old,

27

dark, serious people who had given up hoping for children before David came. He is bright and golden, and they smile at him and shake their heads, then smile at each other and shrug.

My work is simple. I iron, clean up after dinner, wash dishes. I help Mrs. Stern in her sudden fits of cleaning, once a week or so. I meet David at the small private school on top of another hill and walk him home, or take him to his music lessons or his dancing school. I play games with him. I am supposed to help him with his school work, but except for reading I am too far behind to be of much help to him. When he finds this out, he teaches me the multiplication table. Then we do his other homework together, and I catch up, and David's marks improve for a while because he studies for my sake, to teach me.

One day Mrs. Stern does not come down to breakfast. She does not come down for almost a week. I take over the cooking, and something tells me not to ask where she is. Then she comes down again, looking pale. David tells me, "My mother has spells. She gets very sad and doesn't want to see anyone. She just has to be alone until she feels... not so sad." And David looks hurt and alone when he says it, but only for a minute. Then he laughs and makes me smile.

Her spells come about every six weeks, and I get used to taking over. David tries to help. "You mustn't work too hard. It wouldn't be fair." I laugh, because life has never been so easy. I have a room of my own in a beautiful house, with handsome well dressed people who never shout at me. I like handling the fine clothes I iron and the ornaments I dust and the dishes I wash.

Best of all I like dusting the books in Mr. Stern's study. Once he comes in while I am supposed to be cleaning, and finds me reading. He stands there, a squatty little man whose head is always a little bowed. I jump up, but he tells me to sit down again. Then he tells me about his books, about how he wanted to be a rabbi. He shrugs. "But now I'm a businessman, what else could I do? We have to live. And, you know, I'm a very successful businessman." He shakes his head as if he is ashamed. "But I still read a little in the evening. One needn't become a barbarian, eh? Any books you want to read, help yourself. You'll find anything here. I'm catholic in my tastes." He grins and explains the two different meanings of the word. "So we are both catholic in our way," he says, smiling sadly at his little joke.

I shake my head. "I am not. That is all superstition."

"What is?"

28

"All that about God," I answer, thinking of Mama's amulets and Papa's cursing at God.

Mr. Stern is very upset. *"Of course, there is superstition,"* he says, *"but there is still God."* After that he always asks me, to make sure I have gone to mass on Sunday.

Every Friday night I go back to Mama and Papa and stay there until Sunday, going to mass with Mama. The weekend is always the same, Papa silent as he takes my money, Mama smiling and kissing me, saying how she misses me, the last of her children, the baby. *"Well,"* says Papa, *"pretty soon you'll have her all the time. When she leaves school next year she can go work in the factory with you."*

But another law gets in his way. Mr. Stern tells me about it: I must stay in school, the new law says, until I am sixteen. That means I must go to high school for at least two years. David giggles and hugs me and says, *"You see, he'll have to let you stay with us and go to high school."*

High school is more than I have ever hoped for. But knowing that I can go, must go, changes everything. I have seen an opening now, an opening out of the life of my parents and my sisters. I am determined to finish high school and go to college. Somehow I must do it. To stop short of that would be meaningless, just as Papa's great effort has been, for him, meaningless, not taking him far enough to make a new life.

I don't know how I will do it. I must not think too far ahead. My determination sits in my head, in my throat, reaching down into the center of my body. I must. This is, so the teachers say, the land of opportunity. David's parents did not go to college, but David will go. And all my teachers tell me I should go to college. They tell me there are scholarships for poor students who study hard and make good marks. It seems a miracle to me that there should be rewards for doing something so pleasant.

"Oh, you will, you'll do it!" says David when I confide in him. David cannot imagine defeat. Except for his mother's spells, his life has been sunny, a paradise. Because he has been so happy, so loved and petted, he is beautiful and brave, and will try anything. He sings and dances, plays the piano and the violin. He recites poetry and writes little verses of his own. All his talents he parades in front of me as if they exist for me alone, only to make me smile, and when he finally gets a smile from me, he glows with victorious joy. He hugs me and says, *"Oh, Anna, I do love you, don't you love me?"* I laugh

and say, yes, I do.

Everyone, always, all of David's life, turns to stare at his golden beauty, and he wants nothing but to please them. No, he wants one thing, he confides. He will tell me his secret because I told him mine. He wants to be a movie actor. I tell him, of course, he will be a famous actor, and I believe he will.

But I am wrong about that. With all his good looks and talent, he lacks drive, lacks the ability to push others aside and grab something for himself. Years later he tries and fails, tries and fails: four stays in Hollywood during the twenties and thirties come to nothing. Then, during World War II he is offered roles as nazi officers. It seems he is the perfect Hitlerian Aryan: if only he will practice a certain degenerate, sadistic curl of his lip, he can have all the parts he wants. He leaves Hollywood for the last time, and he never mentions acting again.

"You sit there like a queen. Is her majesty receiving?"

Anna looked at the silver-haired, pink-cheeked face poked through the slightly opened doorway, then smiled and nodded.

He pushed the door, making a narrow opening, through which he slid, opening it more with the thickness of his body as it passed through. In one hand he held a small bouquet of flowers and in the other a square package. He was plump and his light suit was tight at the waist, but otherwise he was handsomely, even elegantly dressed, in a fashion not quite American. He even moved in a slightly foreign way. His smile was warm and genuine, but did not express pleasure. It was an expression designed and assumed in order to give pleasure or comfort to others. It was kind, civilized. There was a hint of tiredness in his eyes, but he moved briskly.

"David."

"You say my name uncertainly, my dear, as if you don't quite remember. Are you sure..."

"I've just been reminiscing, remembering high school. I was seeing you in my mind, in those days, and..."

"And then this grizzled old man poked his head through the doorway and you didn't know him." He laughed. "Here, flowers. Look, they come in their own little vase so we needn't call the nurse and face her annoyance." He set the small vase of baby roses on the table next to the bed. "And here's something to pass the time until they let you out of here."

He handed her the small, sharp-edged package, obviously a book. It turned out to be a selection of letters by Bertrand Russell. "I know you've read everything else of his. But this is a new thing they've put together, letters to quite ordinary people like you and me. Did you ever write to him?" Anna shook her head. "You should have, you see. He probably would have answered you and you'd be in this book. You should have written to him anyway. Other people worshipped God and you worshipped Lord Russell, showing, I might say, very good taste."

"Do you know how I first started to read him? It was Mr. Ruggles, remember?"

David nodded. "That high school teacher who got you all the scholarships. I used to be jealous of him because he could do things for you that I couldn't."

"He gave me a pamphlet Russell wrote when he was a pacifist during World War I. I read everything he wrote after that. Up until Mr. Ruggles died we used to meet to talk about Russell's latest book. The last one we read together was *Marriage and Morals,* I think, and Mr. Ruggles thought that went too far. But I defended it. He was a bit shocked; he really was an old fashioned man, about women."

"A bitter man," David said, "if I remember correctly. I suppose he saw all the things he believed in, progress and all that, swept away by the first world war."

Anna nodded. "It took the war to make him see what was already there. While he grew up seeing nothing but progress, my father was being poisoned, body and mind. I suppose the way you perceive the world depends on where you are in it."

"Right. Precisely. You're always right, Anna. Your mind is the same, whatever happened to your memory. The rest of us will go shuffling into senility while you. . . ."

"Still, I owe him everything. Without him I'd have left school at sixteen and led the life of my sisters, the life of everyone else I knew."

"Oh, no, you'd have found a way. You were clearly not the type to just drift into things. You always had the determination to be. . . *Anna Giardino! Stay after class!"*

"Yes, Mr. Ruggles." I sit choking in my chair. The other students turn to look at me. What have I done that is so terrible? It must be the paper I wrote. But it is only the first. If it is so bad, won't I get another chance? Maybe he will tell the principal I can't do high school work, and I will go into the factory with Mama. Papa would like that.

The bell rings. Lunch time. The other students rush out. I go up to Mr. Ruggles' desk. He is stern, gray-haired, the oldest English

31

teacher, and the only man. Yes, he is holding my paper. Well, I won't cry. No matter what he says I won't cry.

"Where did you learn to write like this? It's the only literate paper that's come out of the whole freshman class!" His eyes narrow, and he says, almost accusingly, "You read, don't you." He is praising me! Yes, but he still looks angry. He asks me about myself, who I am, where I live, what my parents do. He listens without comment. Then he begins to talk. He talks and talks.

". . . and I've been teaching here for twenty years. When I started, there were five hundred students in the school and not very many of those were real students. Now there are over two thousand, and anything approximating real education is impossible. The compulsory school law crowds every ignorant fool into my classroom!"

I am too shy to say that, but for the compulsory school law, I would not be here listening to him.

"And this new breed of teachers they are hiring! I don't think many of these ladies have ever read a book, or would ever want to!"

I believe that he must have read every book in the world. And he has seen most countries too. But most marvelous of all, he is a poet. Some years ago he published two books of poetry. He shrugs and frowns as he mentions them.

I begin to stay after class almost every day, eating lunch, going over my papers with him, listening to him talk. He talks about his travels, about poetry, about writing, about books. But always he returns to his obsession, the war, the Great War which has just ended.

"I was born too late. I wish I'd died before I saw it. It's the death of everything. The beginning of the end of everything."

I speak up, for I now read the papers. "Oh, now, it was the war to end all wars, President Wilson said. We will have a League of Nations and live in peace. Women will get the vote soon. And poor people will get education and become. . ."

"Don't parrot slogans! Look at what's really happening. We're already on our way to another war!" He sighs and shakes his head at me. "I have started writing again."

"Poems?" I ask, full of awe.

"No. Not poems. A prose work this time. A survival book. Very practical. These are the days for practical books. This book will tell how to survive in the world as a refugee. What to take when you are forced to leave your home. How to handle police interrogations. Physical fitness in a six by eight cell. Education in a prison camp.

32

Escape techniques. Disguises. A very useful book in the days that are coming."

All the years that I know him, until he dies in 1934, he works on this book. When he dies, his wife says she will keep his manuscript, all his notes, but when she dies only a year later, there is no trace of it.

In my second year of high school, I have another English teacher and see less of Mr. Ruggles. And there are other changes. The Sterns now own three stores and, really rich, they move to Pacific Heights. They want me to come with them, but Papa demands that I move back into the rooms above the store with him and Mama. I know he does it out of fear that I will escape him, and partly out of pure spite.

My sixteenth birthday is coming. Papa has marked the date on the calendar, pointing to it and saying that on that day I will cease to be a parasite on him. I look at the date like a prisoner waiting for execution. I tell David I will have to leave high school. And I tell Mr. Ruggles.

He explodes. He demands to know where I live and walks home with me after school on that very day. He walks up the steep stairs into the dim room where Papa sits by the window. It is like an old drama being played again, like the librarian in Gilroy, like the truant officer. My fairy tale rescuer from the monster, the cruel giant.

I watch Mr. Ruggles and Papa confront each other. Mr. Ruggles is an unlikely looking knight, and Papa is a shrinking giant. For the first time I realize, amazed, that Mr. Ruggles is older than Papa, and both of them look tired, worn. But both are angry, passionate.

"Your daughter is a very intelligent girl, the best student I have had in years. She should finish high school, she must finish, and go on to college. If you do not want to let her do so, there are others who would be glad to take her into their homes, including my wife and me." He adds some vague phrases about courts and guardianship of minors. But his empty threats are unnecessary. I know Papa will collapse. I watch the old fear creep over his face, and I feel ashamed for him. I do not even enjoy my victory because I understand the fear and shame that make him so easy to crush. I have my own share of that same fear and shame.

David adds his help. As usual, it is more practical than threats. He persuades his father to hire me to work in his store on Mission Street. Now I bring home more money than before. My sixteenth birthday passes, and no mention is made of leaving school.

But my last two years at Camino Real High School are gray and

33

dreary except for lunches with Mr. Ruggles and Sunday dinners at the Sterns' big house on Clay Street. Everything else is school, work, homework, with never enough sleep or food. I cannot sleep through the nights when Papa restlessly moans and curses, nor can I eat much sitting across from him at the table. Again, I am spending as much time as possible in the library across the street.

One morning I start my usual walk to school, up over the hill, past the Phoenix Street house, now owned by strangers. I walk past the house, pretending that I am still living there with the Sterns, with David, leaving that lovely house to walk to school, walking down the hill, crossing through the park, down toward the school.

At first I see nothing different. The red brick walls with the long windows are the same. Then I see the people in the street. I wonder why so many students are staying outside the building. As I come closer I see the strangely black look of the windows and the piles of debris on the sidewalks. Then I recognize the damp, smoldering odor that has teased me ever since I woke up this morning, and I know that the high school does not exist anymore, only the shell of it, with nothing inside. My first thought is that Papa has won, and I will be sent to work in the factory with Mama.

Instead I spend the last months of my high school days pleasantly, in tents set up in the park, in the homes of some teachers, Mr. Ruggles for one, who is again my teacher. He has been giving me forms to fill out, and soon after the fire he tells me I have been accepted to the University of California, with a scholarship to pay for books. He has already located a family in Berkeley, friends of his, who will give me room and board for some housework and tutoring their child in English.

Papa makes it easy for me. He calls me a dozen filthy names, accuses me of sleeping with David and with Mr. Ruggles. He says he hopes he will die soon rather than live with the knowledge of such terrible children as he has had. He says he has no children, disowns them all, especially me. He never wants to see me again, and will make sure I never see Mama. With the last bit of strength he has, he pulls my few belongings out of the box beside the couch in the kitchen and throws them out of the window. He watches from the window as I run down and pick up my things. Mama, crying, follows me and helps me pick them up. She pushes them at me, pushes me, and says, "Go." When I try to answer, she shakes her head and repeats, "Go."

I turn and walk away. When I look back, the street is empty. I know

Mama must have run upstairs to care for Papa. His anger will have brought on a coughing fit, and he will need her.

"...penny?"

"What?" Anna shook her head. "Heavens, David, have I been..."

David was smiling. "Daydreaming? Penny for all those deep thoughts."

"You've just been sitting here while I...either I'm unforgivably rude or going senile. But today these...recollections, scenes out of the past...they come at me like..."

"Well, what was it you were remembering, my dear? It didn't look to me like a very happy memory. From your expression, I'd say it was a bit grim."

"I was remembering that last time I left my parents, when I came to your house on Clay Street."

"Oh, yes, I could never forget you standing there on the doorstep, with your clothes draped over your arm, asking to be taken in. We were overjoyed to see you. Mother was in another of her spells, and the servants were so nasty about it. We never got over being intimidated by servants...weren't rich long enough to get used to them. We needed you as much as you needed us. When September came and you went off to Cal, and I to prep school, I think they were relieved to get rid of me, but devastated at losing you again."

Anna sighed. "I'm tired of all this remembering. Dragging along through my life, trying to catch up, to put my mind back together. It's a tiring business. Not being able to remember things is tiring. Confusion is tiring."

"But you remember everything quite well, it seems."

Anna shook her head. "You mentioned my going to the university. Now, you know, I don't really remember a thing about it. I remember the feeling. A steady excitement. Joy. So much to learn, real learning. Answers to be found. Almost religiously. Like heaven, I mean in the physical sense: the Campanile, the lawns, trees, the libraries, the big lecture halls...a little like the heaven Mama believed in. Like a collection of picture post cards, not real, just dream pictures in bright, painted colors."

David laughed. "But, my dear, that's exactly how everyone feels about college days. You needn't have a bump on the head to recall them that way. After all, that's what the university is, except for the people who stayed there for life. It's a never-never land. You step off the world, onto that happy isle where you view the world and discuss it and draw wise conclusions, and read the conclusions others have drawn about it, and then, suddenly, it's all over and you go back to the real world.''

"Is that how you felt?"

"Goodness, no, I hated it. Nothing but study and football games. I was suited for neither. Nice for a short visit, like one of those charming Swiss villages, but not for any long-term stay. I really couldn't think of a thing to do there."

Then, as if David sensed that Anna had had enough of his playful tone, he became more serious. "I suppose I should have been born a woman and you a man. Then I could have made myself attractive and agreeable and been regarded a great success. And you would have been properly admired and rewarded for your abilities, instead of being stuck in a high school for forty years."

"Does that sum up my life?" Anna asked sharply. "Stuck in a high school for forty years. Is that so bad? So useless?"

"Of course not, I didn't say it was useless... just that you were capable of so much more."

"Such as?"

"Well, uh, law... medicine..." David watched Anna's face and looked uncomfortable. "In any field you would have been so... I only meant it seems rather a waste for a woman of your talents to..."

"Why is it that whenever anyone wants to pay me a compliment, he tells me my life was a waste? Why is it better to negotiate divorces or cut out tonsils than to train healthy young minds!"

"Of course, I didn't mean..."

"Money, that's what you meant. I could have made more money. Well, I didn't care about that. I cared about learning, about teaching minds to think. To take a normal ordinary mind and show what it could do... raise it above... to 'polish the jewel of reason'... Mr. Ruggles said that... or was it Bertrand Russell?"

David was nodding anxiously. "Of course, it's not a waste to hold to an ideal, like education. It is a worthy ideal, and you held to it regardless of the difficulties, which is more than I ever did. I have always taken the easy way, the pleasant way. My life, consequently, has been rather tepid. While you can look back on forty years of teaching with pride and the satisfaction of knowing that regardless of the difficulties, you..."

"I can't look back on them at all," Anna said. She laughed, and felt her stiffly earnest face relax. She watched David's face relax like a mirror image of hers. "Not a moment. Really. Do you know that I can't single out and remember one individual student?"

"You will, my dear. See how much you've already remembered. In a few days all the pieces will be fitted in, and your recollection will be complete."

"Will it? Maybe I don't want to remember. So far, what I've remembered hasn't brought me any pleasant feelings."

"Now, now..." David's face looked uneasy again. "That's not like you. You were always Aristotle's perfect human mind, you wanted to know. No matter what it was, you wanted to know. That's why education was so important to you; that's why you became a teacher."

"Aside from the fact that a woman with a B.A. couldn't do anything else in 1928?" snapped Anna, but she was almost smiling.

David nodded, not smiling at all. "Aside from that," he said gently.

"Why did I become a teacher?" Anna was really puzzled. Had she never asked herself this question? She must have, but she could not remember. "Well, of course, there was Mr. Ruggles, what he did. Fighting my father, getting money for me, believing in me. He even had something to do with my getting the job at Camino Real, did you know that? The timing was perfect. I was hired when he retired. He had been grooming me for his job from the time he first knew me. It wasn't easy to get a high school job then. Oh, women were getting the jobs, but only women with connections. I guess he was my connection. And I admired him. I wanted to be like him. He was a teacher. I would be a teacher."

"Simple as that."

"No, there was more. I was at home in the classroom. I was one of those teachers' pets, always raising her hand, eager to give the right answer. I was safe. I always knew what to do. It's not surprising I would come back to the place where I had done so well."

David remained silent, nodding encouragingly, letting her feel her way through feelings, not memories of specific incidents that eluded her, but feelings that remained like rock under shifting, shapeless, transparent water.

"It started in that room behind the barber shop in Gilroy. Learning. I was a learner. It almost didn't matter what I learned. I was excited about taking in anything new. And I had to share it with someone. I couldn't wait to tell someone about a book or... anything, a sight, an idea. Of course, no one wanted to hear, not my sisters, not my classmates. But I needed to give out what I learned. Like a missionary. A fanatic missionary." She looked at David's face. "I'm not making sense."

"Of course, you are. I was just thinking of...of how beautiful you look when you talk that way, how..."

"Don't..." Anna felt herself blushing with shame. "Don't ridicule me."

"My dear, I'm not. Everything you said is...quite wonderful."

"But it doesn't mean a thing to you."

David shook his head. "I've never been...zealous."

"But you were a teacher too, David."

"Oh, that. No, no, the piano and voice lessons were just a means of earning money. A good address, the Clay Street house, for the young ladies to come to and take lessons. It's very profitable to be charming to young ladies, I found. But one doesn't try to teach them much or they get tired, and they get annoyed, and they look for a more charming teacher. No. I gave lessons, and rented out the upstairs rooms, and saved up the money for my next trip. But I know this zeal is in you. I know..." David hesitated. "I know this passion of yours, quite lacking in me, is what I love best in you, though sometimes it gets awfully on my nerves." He laughed.

"It gets on mine too," said Anna.

The nurse walked in on their silence. "It's time to take you down to x-ray," she said. "And then there's the EKG, and...oh, yes, they're going to measure your brain waves. You're going to be a very busy lady." She looked at David as she spoke. He took the hint and stood.

"I'll call you again tomorrow morning." He took Anna's hand and kissed it. It was a perfect act, as though David had invented it himself, at that very moment.

"What a charming man," said the nurse as he left.

Anna did not answer her.

The x-rays done, Anna was left sitting out in the hall, in a wheel-chair, a blanket wrapped around her legs. People walked by, ignoring her. She felt invisible and unreal, as if sitting there in a hospital gown made her less a person than if she wore her clothes. She wished she had brought the book David had given her.

She wondered if Bertrand Russell had answered those letters with the same careful division of topics, the same smooth transitions, the

38

same precise choice of words, and the same unpretentious definitions of difficult words as he had done in his essays. She now regretted never having written to him to tell him she had not only read his essays, but had based forty years of teaching composition on them as models. Not, of course, that her students had written like Russell. She smiled at the thought. But they had learned to introduce a thesis in a short opening paragraph, to begin succeeding paragraphs with a sentence that summed up the topic of each, to carefully define the terms they used, and to provide concrete examples against which they and their reader could check the validity of their statements.

Of course, all that was out of fashion now. Students wrote long, rambling papers, permeated with egotism they mistook for sensitivity and based on a conviction that rules of spelling and grammar were illogical and arbitrary. Well, of course, they were arbitrary; so were traffic lights, but you followed them if you wanted to get where you were going!

She wondered how many papers she must have read and marked through the years. Forty years. Two hundred students each semester. One paper each week from each student. Thirty-eight teaching weeks in each year. Two hundred times thirty-eight times forty...*papers, stacks, miles high, toppling, sagging, crushed, and covered with words, words, an avalanche of scrawled words on tons of paper, coming at me, no, not an avalanche, a tidal wave, growing, rising as it moves on me, coming to bury...*

"They leave you here all day!"

Anna blinked, grateful for the words that had saved her, plucked her out of the hallucination she had almost sunken into. Had she been looking or acting strangely? Had she looked as terrified as she suddenly felt when the image of all those compositions had begun to roll over her mind?

The short, plump woman who had spoken sat in a wheel chair opposite Anna, her tiny feet in jeweled, beaded slippers below her plump legs. She edged her chair closer to Anna and smiled, then sighed. Her broad, golden face was nearly unlined, and her long black hair was thick, but she must have been nearly as old as Anna. Polynesian? Indian? Probably some mixture, like so many of the people in The Mission. "...*and we could give you Senior English out at Lowell High. You've earned it after twenty years of...*"

"*Oh, no, thank you, no,*" I tell the superintendent. "*I would miss the Mission faces.*"

39

He doesn't understand. He thinks all protests, all complaints, are solved by escape. I don't want escape, I want change. But he can't see that, just as he can't see the beauty of the Mission faces.

"So many sick people," said the woman, her dark eyes darting around, then returning to Anna. "You don't think about it till you end up in a hospital."

"You don't look sick," said Anna.

"Oh, I'm not sick. I just twist my ankle. Got to get x-rays. See?" She jutted out a bejewelled, swollen foot. "Did it playing with my grandchild, playing tag around the dining room table. Ashamed to tell the doctor. At my age!" She laughed. Her laugh had a high, light, tinkling quality which subsided into a metallic clucking.

"How many grandchildren do you have?" asked Anna politely.

"Fourteen. Four children, fourteen grandchildren and three great-grandchildren." She said it with a mixture of pride, amusement and weariness. "You a teacher?"

Surprised, Anna looked sharply at the broad, good-humored face. "Retired. I was a teacher."

Another tinkling, clucking laugh. "I can always tell. Teachers and preachers, you can always tell. And I bet you never been married."

"That's right."

"I had a teacher like you. She even look like you. She wore glasses too. She held herself the same way. Even in a wheel chair you... teachers and preachers hold themselves the same way, you know? Why is that?"

"I don't know," said Anna, amused and then thoughtful. "Maybe it has something to do with influencing groups of people. With young people, there has to be a kind of unspoken authority, control. After a while, I suppose it becomes a habit."

The woman was nodding. "This teacher you remind me of. Never forget her name. Miss Hannon. She was strict. Never raise her voice. Never had to. We was all afraid of her. We didn't like her. And, you know something, she didn't care if we didn't like her. All she cared about was, did we learn! No, I didn't like her when I was in school, but now I look back and I think, that Miss Hannon, she made us learn!" The woman shook her head slowly. "It's not like that anymore. Now, they have the new methods. New methods!" She made her lips riffle and rocked her head. "I went to see my little granddaughter at school. Found her in this little room with no desks, just pillows on the floor, and scaffolding the kids are climbing on, and

40

records playing. The Heritage Room, they call it, I guess because it have pictures of Indians and Africans on the wall. That's the new method. And what was little Mimi doing? She had a little map of the world and she was supposed to color different countries different colors. Same exact thing we had to do in school, but with all that noise and everybody climbing the walls. And Mimi having trouble with her reading. No wonder. That's the new methods! Bet you never did nothing like that."

"I certainly did not."

"And I bet you never cared if they liked you or not."

Anna shook her head, then felt uncertain. She did care, but she tried not to let herself care. And some did like her, in spite of her being strict. Some must have. But she couldn't remember any who did. She couldn't remember any at all.

"Why didn't you never get married?"

Anna thought she ought to summon up and send one of her most freezing schoolteacher looks at the presumptuous woman. But it was impossible to feel any offense when she looked at the open, innocent and kindly face. Besides, it was only the same question that had been asked all her life, by nearly everyone she knew even slightly, as if she violated some natural law by not marrying.

"I don't mean you ought to get married. Lord knows, I wished often enough I didn't. I got this man who chased every skirt he ever see and still does, now he over seventy. I work from morning to night to give my children what I never had, but from the minute they start crawling till right now, they nothing but trouble and heartache. I spend my life in church, praying they have good lives, because I can't think of anything else to do, and they just laugh at me and go make all the same mistakes I did, only worse." She had begun to laugh, shaking her head. "I have an aunt once who say, if I had to do over again, I'd have a dog instead!" She laughed harder, wiping the tears from her eyes with both hands. "But I guess I'd do it again, less no one asked me. You never get asked?"

Anna laughed, then shrugged, then laughed again at the image that came into her mind: doughnuts in a bag set against the front door. "When I was in high school, there was a boy. He worked in a bakery, and he used to bring doughnuts and leave them at the front door. He was Italian, like my family, and he spoke to them in Italian and never spoke to me at all. My father wouldn't let any boy near me, but he didn't mind taking the doughnuts. One day there was a note with the doughnuts asking me to run away and marry him."

"But you didn't."

"I was tempted. Just to get away from my father. But that's what so many girls did, and they ended up with a man just as bad as their father."

"That's the truth! And that was the only time. . ."

"No. There was an old friend who wanted to marry me. He was here today visiting. He asked me once, a few years ago, just after my mother died. But he wasn't the marrying kind. Any more than I am. He was just being kind. It would have spoiled everything if we'd married."

"Just the baker-boy and your old friend, nothing in between."

Anna frowned. "A man I met when I was in college. I always thought that if I married anyone, it would be he."

"What happened?"

Anna bit her lip. The question of Arno was too tangled. Of all the memories unreeling in her mind, Arno was one she would be happy to delay examining for a while. Let it stay folded, rolled up, closed. "When I started teaching, they wouldn't hire married women. I had to make a choice."

The woman made a sympathetic riffle with her lips, but the way she shook her head showed that her choice would have been different.

"That rule was dropped a year or two later, but by that time The Depression had come, and they fired women who married."

The woman nodded. "To give jobs to men that was supporting a family."

"I was supporting my mother!" Anna snapped. "And then. . . later, he insisted I give up teaching. I wouldn't. He married someone else." That wasn't the way it happened. Some of the facts were there, incomplete and disarranged, creating a completely false picture. But it was simpler this way, even if it was all wrong, even if it made the woman purse her lips and shake her head, pitying Anna for the wrong things, completely misunderstanding.

The woman went on shaking her head. "If I didn't have my grandchildren, I'd just die. They're your whole life when you get old."

Anna did not try to explain how the thought of making a whole life out of a few children horrified her. That was what had isolated her from most women she had known: their marriages, their children, which seemed to swallow them up. And what about other single women, other teachers she had known? Hadn't there been one or two like her, whose passion was learning, teaching? She could not remember one. There must have been other women who felt as she did, but were they so few and so far spread out that they never...

"This man you was in love with..."

"What man?"

"The one who married someone else."

"Oh," said Anna. "Did I say I was in love with him?" She examined the question as if for the first time. Maybe it was the first time. She shook her head slowly. "You know," she said, not really speaking to the woman, "I don't think I ever really was..."

"Never in love!" The woman's eyes melted with pity.

"I didn't say..."

The nurse had reappeared and was rolling the woman away. The woman made an elaborate, humorous shrug, smiled, and drifted off.

"I didn't say I was never in love," Anna murmured to herself, since there was no one else to listen. *Stephen. Stephen Tatarin. Tall and thin. Skin with high color, almost feverish looking, pink and white. His face floods red, mysterious flood of passion, then turns white again, except for his lips, red lips, too soft for a man, too easily hurt. Eyes a bright, hard blue, a slight oriental turn, some Mongol ancestor in his Russian heritage. He may be very intelligent or just very angry. He sits in my college prep Senior English class. How many will really go to college? We'll see. Not as many as I used to think. After five years of teaching, I began to wonder. Maybe Stephen.*

But after the first week, he is absent. Again. Again. I call his home. "No, I'm not his mother. His grandmother. His mother is sick, in the hospital. Oh, dear, not coming to school. Oh, Dear Lord, what to do with that boy!" She is a tired woman who works in the same factory where Mama used to work, makes a home for her grandson because her daughter is in a mental hospital, Stephen's father has disappeared, and his two sisters are with other relatives. "He's a quick boy, a smart boy, but so hurting over his poor mother and won't speak a word. He's not got enough of the Irish in him. I'm Irish as you can surely tell, but he's a lot dark and broody like his father, Russian. He ought to get an education. He used to read all the time, but now...oh, and I'm trying to save money so he can go to college, but the hospital bills for my daughter and all and all..."

She promises he will come to school, and he does. He sits in the class, staring at me as if his bright blue eyes can send hard rays of bitterness. I face him, look back at him, and he shifts in his chair, turns away from me, gazes hard, out the window as if projecting his mind and soul outside, out, away from me. Some days he sits for the whole class period that way, and I have the strange feeling that, eyes directed out the window, he is perceiving my every move with some other sense.

Finally he turns in an assigned paper. It is a test of me. Two of the pages in the middle are pasted together. I rip the pages apart to read them. This is his accusation: that I would not really read his composition. The accusation fits many other teachers. I am appalled at how many other teachers assign no writing or barely glance at what they assign and collect.

I am appalled, yet I understand. After five years of teaching I sense something happening to me, a kind of erosion, wave after wave of students washing over me, wearing me down. Last summer did not seem long enough. The usual recovery, the eagerness to return, did not come in September. The other teachers tell me I work too hard, must learn to "pace myself," must "develop outside interests." What they mean is that I must learn to hold back, give less of myself, care less, blunt all the edges, the feeling edges that have grown so worn and raw from being rubbed against by so many young people who need so much.

I read Stephen's paper. It is a good paper, though hard and bitter like his eyes. I tell him to study pronoun reference. I suggest some word changes. I mention a book on the subject. I do not let him see that I know he was testing me. I do not tell him that his suspicions are unfair. I pretend not to care, and I almost don't care, because my caring, my feelings don't matter. What matters is that he is here in class, he is doing homework again.

Now he stops looking out the window. His blue eyes are on me all the time. I am constantly being measured, examined by them. His face is closed, a mask. Sometimes it suddenly blushes inexplicably, but I cannot see whether the passionate rush of blood is anger or pleasure or shame. After a long while he begins to flash a sudden smile, instantly trampled by a frown, a rush of color. He seems to have no friends at school. He is good at sports but will not compete. He seems always to be smoldering with an energy barely held, ready to burst out. At first I think the energy is anger, but then I am less sure what it is. Sometimes when he stares at me in the classroom, I feel that his eyes see more deeply into me than others do, more deeply into myself than I do. And more than once, I feel it is I flushing with a rush of hot blood. He sees it! He sees that I blush, and he turns white and shifts in his chair, faces the window. But now there is a curiously peaceful, satisfied look on his face, like triumph, like consciousness of power, like confirmation of some mysterious unspoken pact.

Slowly, so slowly and imperceptibly, like the first start of greening of the dry hills, like a faint odor added to the air I breathe, there begins in me, something, something new in my life. I get up happily on weekday mornings, walking briskly up over the hill from the Bartlett Street rooms I still share with Mama. And in my work, in everything, an enhanced aliveness, a fresh energy even for the worst stacks of papers, the most reluctant students. I move through a clearer, finer air than I have ever known. I move lightly, as if the law of gravity were all but repealed. People begin to smile at me as I walk down the school hulls.

Yet I realize nothing until one night I am shocked awake by a dream, a blatant, naked, sexual dream of Stephen. The joy in our merging bodies is so intense that I still feel it, lying awake in the dark, breathing heavily, seeing everything clearly. Is this what I am? Is this what I want? Am I a depraved seducer of boys? Everything I know, everything I hear around me, every bit of the sense of female sexual evil my father has instilled in me without uttering a word about it, tells me I am evil, depraved, sick.

No. Not everything. Also there are the books, the whole great literature of the world. I have read the books, all the love affairs of literature. I know that none of them was neat, acceptable, conventional, nor, in most cases, fulfilled. Kingdoms fell, men killed one another, women concocted horrifying revenge, all for the sake of love, in the great books. Is this what all of it is saying? That love is irrational, disruptive, mysterious, driving, strong, and as completely absurd as what I feel for this boy?

For now I know that my whole life has come to revolve around him, as if life is a dance I perform for him. I cannot imagine what has kept me alive before I began to love him. And I know, as surely as I know my own true feelings now, I know that he feels the same. Of course. I see, I study, I reinterpret a thousand little gestures and acts, and I know them as revelations of his passion for me. Does he know, or is he still unconscious, as I have been till now? I hope he doesn't know. If he knows, we are in danger. If each of us knows, and knows the other knows... if he makes the slightest move toward me, can I move away, can I do anything but... I must stop this, I must

45

fight against these feelings. But I don't want to fight my feelings. I don't want to fight my happiness.

A bargain, I will make a bargain with myself. A bargain between reason and passion. I will not fight, will not try to deny passion, will know and accept at every moment what I know, that I love this boy, that I am his. But then passion must let reason set the limits of expression. Sublimation. Sublimated love is innocent, after all. Sexual energy can flow through the intercourse of our minds. Sexual energy is, after all, what the saints themselves drew upward to present to their god.

So I reason with myself, so I make the compromises. But the compromises depend finally on Stephen. For if he sees, knows, makes one move toward me, I will forget all compromises.

He knows. The very next day in school I see that he has known for a long time. Our eyes connect once, and he instantly sees that, finally, I know. We both blush and turn away. But not so quickly that I cannot see in the quick turning away, the slow turning back, the lowered eyelids, the sober, quick, soft smile... in all these tiny signs, an agreement has been made, a sacred pact. Now that I have given in, have acknowledged that I am in his hands, he is satisfied. He will do nothing to endanger me, for, of course, the danger is all on my side. This is enough, or, if not enough, not all we want, it is all we can use, and we are lucky to know it.

In later years I see the passion between students and teachers, see the whole drama enacted, sometimes in no more than looks and gestures, sometimes in sad affairs that always end the same: the teacher is reprimanded if male, removed if female or homosexual. And I am so grateful for that luck, or whatever it was, that made and kept our bargain.

For years it is my secret, as it has to be since it is unspeakable.

Later, I could have told, later so much was permissable, or at least mentionable. But by then I know I could not make anyone understand how Stephen and I perfected what we had, protected it, kept it a fine, perfect thing, something that could not be degraded or banalized. No. By later standard such love is unconsummated, unfulfilled, unreal. By later standards, nothing happened between us. So there is nothing to tell. Nothing.

Anna laughed aloud, and the nurse looked startled as she came to push her to another room, to be plugged into machines that took some mysteriously expressed record of the workings of her body. The nurse

46

pulled the tape from the machine and showed it to Anna.

"See, that's what your heart is doing," she said, with the smile she might wear if she were teasing a child.

"Wouldn't it be interesting," said Anna, "if it really told."

"But it does; the doctor will tell you when he reads the tape," said the nurse, as if realizing the child she was teasing was slow witted. She went on explaining as she disconnected Anna from the machine.

Anna did not answer. It was just as well the nurse had misunderstood her, and that she lacked interest in understanding what an old woman said. It had been a lapse on Anna's part to say any such thing to anyone. She had learned long ago to protect herself, to live behind a shield. She could not remember exactly when it was that she began to build the shield. Not at first, not in the beginning of her teaching, for if she had, she would never have loved Stephen. She was now very different from the woman who loved Stephen. Not less passionate. Just better, she thought, at control, at defense. If only she could summon that control against these useless memories...if only she were not so tired.

Anna sighed with relief when they said she could go back to her room. Once there, she slept until a voice woke her. It was Doctor Yogato, standing at the foot of her bed, restlessly poking his fingers in and out of the pockets of his coat. He was dressed more formally, without his white coat, probably, Anna thought, on his way out to dinner or to a party, impatient for this old woman to wake up so that he could be done with her.

"The tests are all right," he said. "Really surprisingly good for a woman your age."

"Then I can leave here now."

"Might as well wait till tomorrow morning, but, yes, I'd say you're perfectly all right. How's the memory?"

"I still can't remember what happened, but everything else is coming back in patches."

"Don't try too hard. Relax."

"How long will it take?"

"You may never remember the incident itself. Often the mind rejects unpleasantness. A form of self-protection."

"I want to remember everything," said Anna. But the almost familiar inner shudder at the thought of that hidden memory contradicted her words. It came and went, leaving her confused and impatient. She may have inhibited many actions in her life, but she

47

was sure she never repressed unpleasant thoughts or memories. She had always faced things. Always.

"Fine, good," said the doctor, nodding at a place just to the left of Anna's head. He was humoring her. And then he was waiting, silently, like a student waiting for her to dismiss him. "Of course," he said, looking at the ceiling as he edged out of the room, "you should call if you have any unusual symptoms: dizziness, nausea...or any questions..."

The door closed. Anna picked up the telephone and called David, who agreed to pick her up as early in the morning as he could.

Then she got up, put her coat on over her hospital gown, and walked down the corridor. She felt stiff and sore. She needed exercise, needed the strengthening movement that would make her quite able to take care of herself when she got home. Already she felt divorced from the hospital. As she passed open doorways and saw people in bed, she viewed them as something different from herself. They were the sick, the victims. She was well. She was only a visitor now. This night might be, she thought, a long one. For a well person, the long, noisy hospital night would be uncomfortable.

But she fell asleep very quickly that night, and plunged immediately into her dream of Camino High School burning. The dream had changed again. The building was a combination of the old one which actually had burned, and the new high school, the one completed just before she started to teach. Each time she tried to identify the building as one or the other, it changed, and she could not be sure which school, old or new, she was in.

But there was an even greater difference. No longer did she stand outside the building, watching the flames consume it from within, while the solid walls stood masking the action of the fire. Now she was inside the building, running through the halls, up the stairs, to her room. She looked around frantically, trying to decide what to save. There were stacks of papers, books, teaching aids, all the things she had accumulated for forty years. Especially precious was the model Globe Theater she and some students had built just before the war. She must save that. But what about the maps of Chaucer's pilgrimage or Huck Finn's river journey? And the papers. The stacks of papers rose to the ceiling.

She grabbed things, right and left, throwing them out of the windows to the street below, crying for people to catch them. But the

48

people on the street only laughed. They were enjoying the excitement of the fire. They were indifferent to her losses. She recognized in the watching crowds, former students, all indifferent, making no move to catch the things she threw down to them.

She decided there was no use in trying to save anything. She jumped from the window and floated three stories down to the ground, a rush of fear going through her like cold air as she floated, but no shock on touching the ground. She felt rather pleased with this feat, and decided to join the crowd, to try to enjoy the fire as an abstract thing, simply fire, beautiful, consuming fire.

But when she looked up, she saw, on the roof above the fourth floor, in the small tiled bell tower, some figures waving to her. She could make out Stephen and David and her mother. There were some others who looked familiar, but she could not name them. They were all waving at her, then lowering their arms and looking at the flames climbing up toward them. She began to shout at the people around her, point to the bell tower, but they were all as indifferent as they had been toward the things she threw out the window.

"Jump!" she cried. "Jump! I did, and I wasn't hurt." But they did not seem to hear her. She screamed and screamed at them to jump, but they looked blankly down at her. They seemed to be waiting for her to do something. Finally she understood, and while the crowds around her watched indifferently, she ran up the front steps, pulled open the heavy metal door, and ran into the flames.

WEDNESDAY

DAVID DROVE STRAIGHT up the Twenty-third Street hill as if it were a clear, level road. His little sports car rumbled deeply, and he looked as if he enjoyed hearing its smooth, even roar as it climbed. He always listened attentively to his motor and said that after listening to faltering music students all day, he knew the sound of his motor was the only true music in his life.

To Anna, all his cars, throughout his life, sounded and looked the same, except for slight color changes. Lately, however, as David grew older, his cars grew more fanciful, more like toys. This one, lovingly stored throughout his stay in Europe, was a low, long convertible, like a racing car, and completely unsuited to driving around in San Francisco fog. Anna pulled up her coat collar and hunched her shoulders. The wind, the roar of the throbbing motor, and David's voice came to her in muffled gusts.

He made a quick turn on Phoenix Street (his driving had become playful too) and stopped in front of the house. "And here we are." He looked up at the house. "The place is older...like us all."

"It must seem strange to you," said Anna, "every time you see it, the house you grew up in, cut into three apartments and owned by your former maid."

David winced, then wrinkled his nose at Anna's referring to herself as a maid. "Not at first," said David. "When I came home after the war and found you here, I never thought about it at all. I'd seen Europe; that was all I thought about. But lately I think more about the old place." He grinned. "Sign of age." He climbed out of the car and came around to help Anna out. Actually she needed the help less than he. "Absurd," said David, "for a creaky old man like me to still be driving one of these things. I must go on a diet or one day I'll get stuck in the thing and have to be pried out."

50

Anna was looking up at the house. "I've let it deteriorate so, I'm ashamed to have you see it. These past few years..."

"I was surprised you didn't sell it when your mother died. All these steps...really as silly as my car for people our age."

They started up the stone steps, cut between the two high, cracked concrete walls. The steps slanted unevenly, a few stones chipped or tipped. Anna said, "These steps have become dangerous. I really must..." Then she remembered that she had thought or had said she really must do something about them during hundreds of other climbs over many years.

At the top of the steps they surveyed the front garden. The trees needed pruning and the wild grass was choking out the last remnants of flowering bushes. "I've let the garden go wild. I've been meaning to...,"

"What's that?" David pointed to a sheltered spot next to the house, where green shoots poked up in short rows.

"The couple in the rear apartment. They plant seeds, then lose interest and the weeds take over before I ever find out what they planted." She looked closer. "But they're doing better this time. That's definitely lettuce, and carrots in the third row. Lori. I rented the place to Lori," Anna said, slowly and carefully outlining her memory, nodding slightly in approval at getting it right. "A nice, quiet girl, a waitress with an M.A. in philosophy. Some time or other, I'm not sure just when, her friend Lorenzo moved in with her. Lorenzo is the gardener. I don't think he does much else. Lori says he writes, but I seldom hear the typewriter. He's got terribly long hair, what there is of it. He's nearly bald. Lori dotes on him."

David was laughing as they climbed the short flight of wooden steps up to the big front porch. "I love your little dry descriptions of people Remember how you used to tell me about the students, and the other teachers...who was that one who drank...when you first started teaching? Oh, my sides would hurt from laughing."

Anna shrugged. She didn't remember.

The big front door that Anna had faced so many years ago stood wide open, exposing a bare, shabby foyer. Anna's apartment covered the second floor. Her mother had lived in the first floor front apartment until she died, and the rear apartment, where the young gardeners now lived, was always rented to someone.

They walked through the doorway and started up the long flight of steps. "Who's in your mother's apartment now?"

51

Anna stopped on the fourth step. "Isn't that funny? I can't remember."

"Well, you let Arno Steadman use it for a while after your mother died, and then..." Anna stiffened. "No. Is it Arno? Still there?" David had stiffened too, with disapproval. Anna could feel it although she kept her face averted and did not answer.

An answer came anyway, as the door below them opened and a deep but querulous voice called, "Anna. Is that you, Anna? What in hell happened to you?"

The man in the open doorway below them was very tall and thin. He was about Anna's age, with light skin and thick, white wavy hair. His moustache was darker, almost black. He leaned in the doorway with unconscious assurance, the ease of a man who had once been very handsome. He looked up and, seeing David with Anna, his lip curled slightly. He gave a sharp, jerky nod in David's direction, and David returned an almost identical gesture, neither of the men actually looking directly at the other. *"Yes, Arno, I am. I'm pregnant, and all your shouting won't change that."*

"I thought you were an intelligent woman, who..."

"Stop it! I'm not asking you to marry me. I have six months to go before I get my teaching credential, and I have Mama to support. I won't have the baby, I won't be any trouble, but I need help, I need..."

He goes on shouting, like an innocent man on whom I have put a curse, an intolerable and sordid sin of my own. He stuffs money into my hand, then shouts again and again that he "cannot handle something like this!"

And so it is David who makes the squalid inquiries, who borrows the family car and drives me over Twin Peaks, between foggy sand dunes, to the gray stucco house, from which I hear the ocean while...

Damn! A useless memory, Anna thought, determined not to give this scene space in her head. Millions of women had had abortions, and contrary to all the stories, they were not the most important experiences in their lives. Anna had neither suppressed this memory nor worried over it, ever. She could see no reason for dwelling on it now.

Yet she could see that, as far as these two men were concerned, the abortion might as well have taken place yesterday. Arno and David had had little contact with each other over the years and probably hardly ever thought of each other. But confronting each other today, they were back in that place again, David hating Arno with all the idealistic passion of a seventeen-year-old, and Arno, defensive, ready to claim that, after all, he had given Anna the money, but there were certain things he couldn't cope with.

Arno glared at her, a silent, infuriated demand that she account for herself.

"You didn't hear what happened?" asked Anna.

"Only what was in the stupid newspaper," Arno grumbled.

"You could have telephoned the hospital," said David, "and they would have given you more details. They would even have put you through to Anna; she had a phone in the room. Then you would have been reassured, and not worried about her." David's voice was smooth and kindly. Anyone who did not know him would not have suspected the fury in it. Anna suppressed a smile.

Arno did not even look at David, much less answer. He gave a little shrug as if to shake off any implication that he should have shown more concern for Anna. He looked at her as if he were getting ready to forgive her for troubling him. "So, you're all right."

Anna nodded. "I'm all right."

"My damned prescription ran out, right when I was laid up with the pain, and then another migraine hit me. I couldn't get down the damned stairway, and I'd run out of tea!" he concluded in a burst of indignation.

"Arno's developed very bad arthritis," Anna explained to David, who was looking at her with a carefully expressionless face.

"Perhaps you want me to go to the store for him," said David.

"No, what's-her-name finally went for me," Arno said, waving one hand toward Lori's apartment. "Well, stop making me crane my stiff neck at you, come down here and tell me what's happened to you. Kettle's on." He turned his back and walked quickly into the apartment as if he had no doubt they must obey his summons.

"I'd better be going. . . ."

Anna grasped David's hand firmly, shaking her head. "No, come in and have a cup of tea with us." They walked back down the few steps together and into Arno's apartment.

David stood looking around the front room. "Everything's still the same as when your mother lived here!" Anna's eyes followed his. There was the small sofa, the little tables with carved legs, all cheap imitations of different periods. On every table and chair, on the back of the sofa, even on the mantel piece above the big fireplace (this apartment had been the old living room) were crocheted doilies. David touched one and smiled. "Makes me almost see her, sitting in the rocker, crocheting." On the walls were small framed photographs, brown and faded: Anna's parents' wedding picture, baptismal pictures of their children, overexposed snapshots of relatives in the Old Country. David examined them all, then turned toward the window. "Where's the rocking chair?" He frowned at the books and papers scattered throughout the room and piled high on a card table which stood where the old rocking chair had been. A straight chair stood at an angle from the table, as if hastily pushed back. "Arno still writes," he said.

"Yes, the old *Socialist Liberation* still carries his column."

"No more," Arno shouted from the kitchen. "They finally folded last month."

"Sit down, my dear." David led Anna to the sofa and pushed aside some papers, revealing tea stains and cigarette burns. He frowned.

Anna stared at a drooping, soiled, crocheted grape cluster on the arm of the chair as if seeing it for the first time. "I've been meaning to figure out what to do with all Mama's things. Meanwhile I let Arno use the place for a while."

David sniffed and raised an eyebrow. "Let's see," he said innocently, "your mother died . . ."

"Eight years ago," said Anna. She frowned, puzzled at the length of time. Yes, it was eight years. She pretended not to see the disapproving shake of David's head, though he was surely right to disapprove. Eight years. Where had they gone?

"And here I am," said Arno, taking long but slow strides into the room, "living among dusty antimacassars because she won't let me throw away any of this junk. There are even some of her mother's old clothes in the closet. I didn't know you were around," he said, suddenly turning toward David.

"I was in Europe for three years. I just got back."

"I thought it was permanent."

"It is. I'm just back to settle a few things and sell the Clay Street house."

Anna had been absorbed in looking around at all her mother's things, soiled, dusty or lying under Arno's books and papers. But at this she turned toward David. "You're going to do it, then?"

David nodded. "I found the place. In the south of France, near the Italian border, very close to where your people came from. Living is cheap there, and I've made friends. As soon as I've settled things here I'll go back."

"For good," said Anna.

David smiled. "I told you I was going to settle down and stop traveling."

"Nice living, if you can afford it," said Arno.

"I have a bit. Enough to last my time," said David, "and still manage not to sponge off my friends." His tone was clearly accusatory, like the silence that followed. "I'd better go."

This time Anna did not try to stop him. "Thank you, David. Thank you for..."

"I'll call you tomorrow and see how you're getting on. And, of course, if you need anything..."

There was a long silence after he was gone. Then Arno smirked and said, "Good old David."

"Yes," said Anna firmly.

"Gotten a little plump, hasn't he, more cherubic than ever. He looks in good shape, though, not falling apart like me. Oh, well, old fairies never die, they just..."

"Don't talk that way about David," Anna snapped.

"Well, I didn't say anything against the old..."

"That's enough! You'll leave David alone."

"What's got into you? What are you yelling at me for? You go off in the middle of the night, get yourself into a mess, and then the moment you're home you're mad at me!" After a moment of silence he added, "Still, that's better than the way you've been. We hardly exchanged two words in the past six months." He handed her a cup of tea. "Are you all right?"

"Yes, except I can't remember things."

"What things?"

"I didn't remember that you were here, until I saw you. Then I remembered back when..." She almost told him she remembered the abortion, but it was absurd to bring up something that happened so many years ago, to altogether different people. "....things from years ago. The doctor says I'll be all right."

"You still don't remember what happened?"

"No." She frowned and waited, half-expecting that memory finally to come, but all she felt was an uneasy chill that made her shiver.

"Have you seen today's paper?" When she shook her head, he went to the card table and pulled a newspaper out from under the pile of papers. He stood in the middle of the room, cleared his throat and began to read aloud.

DARE WE WALK THE STREETS?

For some time this paper has attempted to draw attention to the lack of safety in our city. A recent incident shockingly illustrates the growing hazard of a simple act of leaving one's house after dark. Miss Anna Giardino, sixty-eight, retired after forty years of service in our schools, was found on the street near Camino Real High School, in the Mission District, where she has lived since childhood.

Apparently her spirited defense discouraged a would-be attacker, and Miss Giardino's injuries were not serious. She was fortunate. Others have been beaten, robbed, sometimes killed. It is a sad commentary on our civilization when our old people, after having earned, through long service to our community, rest and security, find themselves in an increasingly violent city, prey of prowlers who should be caged like the savage animals they are.

And who are these prowlers but the end product of decades of coddling, permissiveness in our schools whose falling standards creates the moral dry rot that infects our public institutions at every level. . .

They were both laughing too hard for Arno to finish. "It sounds as if whoever wrote that thinks I got what was coming to me," Anna said, "since I'm clearly one of those permissive creators of moral dry rot, whatever that is."

Arno sighed. "It's not really funny."

"No, it's real, the violence." Anna nodded slowly. "No doubt I was attacked by some young hoodlum, a beginner, practicing on old ladies. Probably one of my own students. Yes, that's occurred to me. It's possible. It's quite likely, isn't it?"

"Anna. . .that's an ugly look on your face. I don't like it. You're afraid."

"Why should I be afraid?"

"I don't know. But I don't think I've ever seen you afraid before."

"Well, maybe I am afraid. Of not being able to remember. Afraid my mind is going. Afraid of becoming senile and helpless. But. . .I'm afraid of. . .I think it was someone who knew me. I think someone wanted to hurt me." There. She had said it. She had let herself think it.

"Bullshit. . ."

"Students, sometimes parents, have been known to attack teachers, even to kill them."

56

Arno sniffed. "You're letting your imagination..."

"I keep trying and trying to remember. But all that comes to me are old memories, things I don't care about anymore, things I'd rather forget."

Arno leaned back and stroked his moustache. "How would you feel if you discovered it was one of your own students who attacked you?"

Anna thought for a minute, then felt the edge of her lip twitch. "Not as bad as I'd feel if I discovered it was one of my own students who wrote that editorial!"

Arno laughed. "Well, that's better!" He took the tea cups and put them on the table next to the sofa. "I've had a devilish couple of days, I'll tell you." He spoke as if what had happened to Anna had no importance except as an inconvenience to him. "I've been working on an article that will expose..." Yes, he had forgotten all about her now and would talk about himself for as long she would listen. "*...so the only thing for it is socialism, you see that. You have to. Anyone with half a grain of sense can see that if you take...*"

I sit listening to Arno, who goes on without waiting to hear whether or not I agree with him. I mop up drops of spilled coffee with a paper napkin, but it is futile. The stains are too deep and dark in this coffee-clogged table in this dear, dingy cafe. Classes are exciting, but walking across the campus and down here to sit, to argue, to listen, is almost more exciting.

Arno is exciting. So completely different from anyone I know, like a man from another planet. Arno makes me understand what it means to be poor, for he is not poor. He is so far removed from poverty that when he talks about abolishing poverty, he sounds as if he is talking about abolishing a strange, foreign odor. When I listen to him, I know myself, I know all the poverty-stricken parts of myself that I want to hide from him: the insecurity, the self-doubt, the uncertainty with words and ideas. No matter how many books I have read, there is still the deep diffidence, the shame, like the shame and fear of my parents, lost in a strange country. I am determined to wipe out that shame, not to be afraid, if it is the only thing I do in college. But not to forget it. I must remember it if I am going to teach, to help others wipe it out.

But I will never be like Arno. Even David is not like Arno. In David's house there are money and books, but not this security, not this assurance. The Sterns are Jews, after all, never quite unafraid, always straining a bit. But Arno comes from five generations of Anglo-Saxons in America, three of those generations in California.

57

His value has never been in question. He is fearless because he has never known what there is to fear.

". . . and if my crazy father hadn't squandered all the family money in his muddle-headed schemes, I wouldn't be broke and wondering what in hell to. . ." But he can't be broke. Or is being broke different from being poor? He doesn't juggle part-time jobs, and he talks about going to Europe for a year after graduation, to live in Paris and write. By broke he means not rich anymore.

". . . you haven't read Shaw?! Listen, Anna, my girl, you're not to speak to me again until you take this home and read it, with special attention to Act Two. That wraps it all up, tells it all, and if you're not a perfect fool, you'll be able to see that. . ." He always makes me feel like a fool, giving me that wide-eyed, stunned look when I admit I haven't read something. But he doesn't mean to be arrogant, and he isn't really a snob. *". . . because it's clearly too progressive for The Chronicle, and if I don't find a publisher by. . ."*

Anna stood. "I want to go upstairs now. I'm very tired." Arno stopped talking, looking puzzled and then offended. He did not even go to the door with her.

She climbed the stairs slowly. By the time she got to the top she felt better. It was the talking that had tired her. Physically she was all right. Still, as soon as she got the door open, she went straight to the rocking chair, the one David had missed from the apartment downstairs. It was the only thing of her mother's that she had moved, bringing it upstairs and setting it near the window where she could look across more rooftops all the way, on a clear day, to the tip of the towers of the Golden Gate Bridge.

She sat down, keeping the rocker still. As soon as her body fit into its curves, she remembered this posture as a habitual attitude, this sitting before the window, stiffly, in a non-rocking rocking chair. It surprised her. She had never been able to sit still for long. She thought on her feet. She walked long distances. She'd even sold her car after her mother died because she no longer had any need for it. She preferred to walk. That was why, probably, she was seldom stiff, except for those first few morning moments. What a bore it was, sitting, except for a short rest, or perhaps to read.

Anna's front room had been the Sterns' bedroom, the room where heavy drapes darkened it as a shelter for David's mother during her spells. It was a long, high-ceilinged room with a fireplace and six tall windows on two walls. Next to the front room was a small dining room, then an even smaller kitchen. In back there were two bedrooms and a bathroom, the original bathroom, completely unchanged and as big as one of the bedrooms. The house had been partitioned hastily, during World War II. Partitions sliced through rooms without regard to proportion. Ornate ceiling trim was cut off suddenly by a wall, then flowed on behind the wall through the next room. Some rooms seemed taller than they were wide. The huge window in the kitchen was completely out of place, even dangerous, beside the sink where someone might slip and go crashing through. It, and a similar window in one of the two bedrooms, had two bars across it for safety.

Anna looked around the front room as if she were looking at someone else's apartment. Aside from the rocking chair, the only furniture was a footstool, two small straight chairs, and two reading lamps. Two walls held filled bookshelves, clear to the ceiling. There were low bookshelves under the windows, and even a line of books across the mantelpiece over the fireplace. The shelves had grown, haphazardly, to hold the growing accumulation of books. The place was devoid of ornaments, almost of furniture, but it contained every book she had ever owned, from her high school textbooks to recently bought paperbacks. She knew that she should get rid of some she would never look at again. But at the thought of selling or throwing away books she felt overcome by a sense of dread like that of a deeply religious person who is asked to throw away a sacred relic.

She got up and began to wander through the apartment, looking at the packed shelves. The front room and dining room contained all the books she owned by the end of the war, when she bought the house: all her school books, including her set of Shakespeare, her second hand classics, everything Bertrand Russell had written since 1915. She had kept even the useless education texts she was forced to buy while earning her teaching credential. All these books were musty-colored and hardbound, except for the ones under the dining room window, the dry, cracked and nearly brown-paged paperbacks she bought during the forties, during the war, when cheap pocket-books, as they were called, first became available. *"Mysteries! Detective stories! Really, Anna!" Arno laughs.*

I laugh too. "I don't seem to be able to concentrate on anything, can't read anything else. It's the war, everything so wild, so hectic. When it's over, and things settle down . . ." That's all we talk about: when it's over, when it's over . . .

Arno comes in at all hours of the day and night, whenever he can leave the Presidio where he is stationed, waiting to be sent out to the Pacific. Every leave-taking is a passionate farewell, in case this time is the last...but he is never sent out. We spend all our free time together, planning, hoping...when it's over...when it's over. Love and peace and happiness...when it's over.

But when it's over, nations go back to their more usual, lower-keyed hostilities, and Arno goes back to his wife in Baltimore. I stop reading mysteries and try to deal with the harder mysteries of my life. Or try to forget them, in reading, in teaching.

Anna moved through the kitchen toward the hallway, noting as she passed that most of the shelves also held books. Except for one cupboard, which was large enough to contain the amount of food that interested Anna, food and utensils had been crowded off the shelves by science fiction books, the only novels which, during the mid-fifties, had seemed to Anna to be based on anything like a moral sense. She went on into the hall, lined mostly with biographies and collections of letters, the sociological and political memoirs she read after the war, and all the books about The Bomb and what it would mean to live in a world that might be blown up at any moment. There was more Bertrand Russell here, and there were gaps where Arno had borrowed books since he moved in.

She stood in the doorway of the small bedroom she slept in. A narrow bed stood in the corner and there was no rug on the polished wooden floor. The shelves in this room held an excellent collection of recent books on racial and ethnic problems. Of course, Richard Wright and Dubois were in the front room along with earlier writers. This room was what Arno had once referred to as her post-Baldwin room: "...after James Baldwin, the deluge."

Anna's eyes roved the book titles, then suddenly stopped, focused, stuck on one bright red book titled BLACK DEATH. *Assembly. The schedule is upset, again, again, the precious minutes chopped off each class, a disordered, distracted hum in the air, because we are to have an assembly today. Again. I dread the noise, the chaos in the huge auditorium which is the heart of the main building, rising through the center of three storeys, big enough still to contain the entire student body, though now it has become risky to pack them in all together. Riots. Confusion. Danger. Usually we split them up, have two smaller assemblies, close the balconies, hope to contain their fierce, abandoned energy in smaller groups.*

But today's speaker, the famous author of BLACK DEATH, has little time to spare for us while he passes through San Francisco. He can speak only once, briefly, and would not have come at all except that Camino Real High School is his alma mater.

I remember him well. One of the few pre-war Negroes of San Francisco, graduating during the war. He was light tan and he spoke with a clipped accent that set him apart from the rest of the students, set him apart from me. Like my students, I speak with a Mission accent that Arno says sounds like Brooklynese, the result perhaps of the same mix of Irish, Latin, Jewish accents. Arno has asked when I will finally lose that accent, and I tell him, "Never, I hope!"

But Gregory, my student who has become a famous author, never spoke with a Mission accent. He imitated Movie English accents and used long words, often incorrectly. I did not like him. He was grade-conscious and ambitious, but had little curiosity, as I remember. Worst of all, he was a snob, particularly toward the Blacks who began coming from the South in large numbers during his senior year. I remember that he would have nothing to do with them, and I very distinctly remember the time I heard him refer to one as "straight out of the bush."

He competed in contests: patriotic essays for the American Legion, speeches about economic opportunity for the Mission Lions Club. He had one set speech that he gave over and over again, about America offering equal opportunity to all who were willing to work hard. I used to watch his eyes for a sign of irony. But there was none. He told these businessmen, who would not hire him to work in their shops, what they wanted to hear.

I think I understood his fear and shame, but I could not help but despise him. I agreed grimly when my colleagues said he would go far, but we heard nothing of him after he graduated, nothing for almost fifteen years.

Then his book was published, his supposedly autobiographical novel, about his ghetto childhood in San Francisco. It was a grim story, the standard struggle of a sensitive young talent surviving rats, hunger and prejudice. But I know his mother was housekeeper for a rich Pacific Heights family, neighbors of David. My student grew up in their mansion, and they sent him through college. No matter. Perhaps the book isn't really a lie. It was the truth for so many other poor Blacks. Maybe he has been chosen as the voice for them, and it doesn't matter whether or not he really lived the life he claims to have lived. Perhaps if he had lived it, he would not be able to write it. I am ready to give him every chance. I am glad he is famous, glad his book is a best seller, glad the school and all the young people in it can point to something fine, famous, admired, coming out of Camino. It would be so good for my students, it is just what they need now, if he should give his little Lions Club speech, in a new version, to them, telling them to study, learn, work hard. The speech was a lie when he gave it twenty years ago, but it is not quite a lie now. Whatever chances my students have now, and there are more chances, they must learn, if they are to be able to grab those chances. Even if he only tells them to work for grades, as he did, he might do some good. Even if he tells them to put aside their narcotics—their drugs and music and sex and noise—only for the sake of ambition, money, even that would be something. I am hopeful for the smallest nudge toward the discipline that might help them struggle out of the power of the forces that will kill them, the way my father was killed, but more seductively, so that they never face the enemy head on. I can't wait for the revolution, like Arno. I can't sigh and say, "When we have socialism . . ." the way Mama sighs and says, "Soon, I go to heaven . . ." I must do something, for some of them, if only for a few of them, now. Now. And he will come out to them now, not the prig I knew him to be, not a person at all, but a symbol that might spur them on, might give them the hope that will make them learn, at least, to read.

Flag salute. Relative quiet. We sit down in expectant hum and rustling. There he comes.

I would never have known him. His hair stands out a foot around his head. He wears a dashiki covered by a leather vest, and there is . . . yes, there is a match hanging out of the side of his mouth. No matter. It is only a fashion, a mannerism. Not important. Maybe it is a clever touch. He dresses like the toughest, like the ones without hope, and they will feel closer to him, they will listen when he tells them there is hope. A clever touch. A good touch. I take back all my mean old thoughts about him. I lean forward to listen.

And I hear a diatribe of hate, a call for violence, an indictment of all institutions, especially schools, a labeling of all whites as "racists" and a confused eulogy to "my black grandmothers." All this is delivered at the top of his voice, in an accent thicker than any I ever heard from southern Blacks coming during the war, the Blacks he would not speak to then.

The white students clap languidly, the Mexicans, with more enthusiasm mixed with a sort of mocking, reckless laughter. The black students cheer, sigh, laugh, gasp, punctuate his every phrase with a shouted slogan. It is like a revival meeting at which the congregation rocks and cries, "amen, amen," to each statement, screaming and crying until they have whipped themselves up into a blind ecstasy. I watch the faces of a few other teachers. The black ones are shouting with their students, looking from time to time uneasily over their shoulders, as if to make sure they are noticed by their students. The white teachers nod, wearing smiles as a wooden dummy in a store window wears clothes.

And now I know him, I recognize him now. I know he has not changed at all. He is still the same ambitious, self-hating prig he has always been. With no knowledge of these young people, with no concern for their needs, he is doing whatever will stir them, will give him his success, will make the grade. If the fashion should go back to minstrel shows and soft shoe dances and shuffling incoherency, he will learn that too. I still pity him. I think I understand him too. But I do not approve. I cannot condone.

I get up and walk out. Everyone sees me, all the way up to the second balcony.

Later a black teacher nudges me in the hall and murmurs that I was right to walk out on "all that crap." But he never lets himself be seen talking to me again.

There are three serious fights the next week, near riots, reviving racial tensions, wiping out truces that had held for a long time. Vandalism rises. It takes over a month before the students begin to settle back down to their usual level of distraction and confusion. With one addition: a smoldering look that accuses me of racism.

I am sixty. I could retire now. I should, I must. But to leave now would be to abandon them to the mentality that dominated that assembly. To leave now would be to be driven out, defeated, broken. No. I will hang on to the mandatory age. Hang on and fight to the end. Fight whom? For what?

Leaning on the door jamb, Anna turned away from the packed shelves. Perhaps the doctor was right: there are some things a person does not want to remember.

Passing the bathroom, she glanced at her collection of poetry, the most recent of her acquisitions, stacked on an old vanity table. She was still uncertain with poetry, almost as uncertain as her students had been. But Arno had helped. In those months after her mother died, he often read poetry aloud, sometimes his own, which she did not like because it seemed harsh and tight, like brief signals of feelings withheld. But when he condescended to read Whitman to her, she felt that she could understand poetry and might, in her old age, stop feeling stupid when she opened a book of verse. Reading Whitman was like taking one of her long walks in the sunshine, with the wind in her face.

The larger bedroom, which had been her room during her last year with the Sterns, she used as a study. Here was a strange mixture of the reading she had done during the past ten years. There was a large group of religious books that she had bought to read to her mother, most in Italian. There were current novels, but more historical works and many philosophy books. Most of them were unread. Either she kept them only to read to her mother or she had bought them for herself and lost interest or energy after the first chapter. So often, in her later years of teaching, she had been too tired after reading a set of papers to do any reading for herself. This room, her study, her own workroom, ironically, contained books that were strangers to her.

In the corner in front of a long window was her huge desk, an old classroom desk salvaged from the school basement during her twentieth year of teaching. The desk had stood unused since she retired, and boxes were stacked around it and on it, so high that they cut off almost all light from the window. She stood near the desk, touching one of the boxes, feeling the fine, dry dust come off onto her fingers. *"Take anything you want," Stewart Warner says, "The janitors will remove the rest." His face is bland, as always throughout all the years, bland as when he calls me old-fashioned, bland as when he stands there nodding benevolently at students no matter what they say.*

"This represents a lifetime of work," I tell him. "Someone must be able to find something here of use to . . ."

The bland, nodding face confronts me like a stone, a blank denial. It is a life's work, and no one wants it anymore, just as they don't want me anymore. "Anything you want. . ." he repeats, with a vague gesture sweeping across the stacks of papers, books, charts.

"I'll take it all!"

They stuff everything into boxes. They send a group of students in a station wagon. The boys carry the boxes up the stairs, cursing openly at the long climb, not caring that I hear them. When they leave, they will laugh at me, the senile, mean old teacher who cannot part with all the junk left from her outmoded old teaching. Watching them leave I feel ashamed.

But now Anna thought it might have been a lucky thing that she kept everything. She would sort through it before she threw it all away, and the sorting would help her remember, like sorting through all the years that were lost, working her way up, finally, to last Sunday night.

She was even curious about what she had saved. What did one keep during forty years of teaching? Forty yearbooks? No, she had stopped saving yearbooks after the first ten years, had gotten rid of all but the first one. As if called by her thoughts, the 1929 yearbook was immediately visible, its end sticking up over the edge of one of the dustiest boxes. Its cover was limp and cracked, its pages surprisingly full of words, instead of the photographs that took up most of the space in later yearbooks. But that was the only difference, she thought, as she turned the shiny, heavy, brown-edged pages, too thick and pretentious and permanent for the feeble sentimentalities printed on them. A high school yearbook was not a book at all, but a list of banalities in very strict form, like the sentimental religious pictures the nuns used to pass out, trying to bribe her to come to catechism. Form and content, indistinguishable whether from 1929 or 1969. A few changes of hairstyle or fashion made no real difference. The yearbook was as far removed from the reality of the school and the world as were the pink and gold images of the smiling Virgin Mary.

Anna set the old book down. Maybe there was something to be said for hazy or even falsified views of the past. Why should she remember every detail of those forty years of teaching? Most people did not, even people who had not been hit on the head. This seemed like wasted, tedious work, filling in memory gaps only to turn away finally and forget them again.

She bent over the boxes, and, by pushing things one way and another, was able to get a general idea of what she had kept. One box contained her model of the Globe Theater, still in good condition though over thirty years old. Twice a year for thirty years, she set out the Globe and explained, and helped the students imagine. Then it was pushed aside, along with the chairs, and the room became a theater, everyone reading and acting, with special gusto each time they killed Julius Caesar.

There were boxes full of books, out-of-print, obsolete textbooks, each of which contained at least one essay, story or rhetorical explanation that should not be lost to her students. There were three old grammar books, one of them her precious Tanner: clean, complete, classic, no pictures, no colored print, nothing to make grammar a game, just a beautiful, honest book—out of print after 1940.

The last two boxes were more recent. They contained mimeographed and dittoed lessons. She felt uneasy as she looked at them, stacks and stacks of papers. Why did she have these from only her last few years? Well, of course, in the early years there were no duplicating machines. But even if there had been, she would have thrown away everything year by year. She never could stand to do the same thing twice in exactly the same way. There were always changes, until those last few years when it did not seem worth the trouble to change, to think through a new lesson, to study new material, and she began to use the old things again and again. "Why shouldn't I!" she muttered. "Wasn't it hard enough just coping from day to day? No one cared. They didn't want to learn. What was the difference whether I...I couldn't anymore, that was all. I was tired. A person gets tired..."

She stood upright, stiffened, clamping her mouth shut. Old people who live alone begin to talk to themselves, aloud, she thought. Soon they mutter all the time, unaware of what they are doing, not understanding why people stare at them in the street and why children laugh.

She took a deep breath, then bent over again and picked up one of the lightest boxes of mimeographed sheets. She carried it to her front door, leaving the door open as she went down the steps, out through the big front door and down to the garden. She walked around the side of the house toward the garbage cans and almost tripped over the two young people before she saw them, kneeling over their little vegetable garden.

Anna looked over the box hugged to her chest, directly down on Lorenzo's bald pate. The long fringe of hair around it had fallen over his face. Lori's long, straight black hair fell forward from her bent head, like a veil. But both curtained faces evidently could see the world they were hidden from by their hair. Lori jumped up.

"Miss Giardino! We heard you were in the hospital!"

"I was. I just got home."

Lorenzo got up more slowly and took the box from her hands. Anna felt herself lose balance along with the loss of the weight of the box. She leaned unsteadily forward and then to the right. Lori took her arm.

"I'm all right. I just wanted to dump some trash." She realized she sounded ridiculous and felt furious. The young could be impulsive, but the old, making sudden decisions and acting on them, were only foolish. "I came home, and I saw that stuff lying there and I couldn't wait to get rid of it." Now she felt even more angry. Why should she explain herself to them?

Lorenzo looked at her and then at the box, which he took across the garden and set beside the garbage can. Lorenzo hardly ever spoke. It was Lori who said, "Looks like old papers from school."

Anna nodded.

"Wow, that's brave," said Lori. "My mother's a teacher and she keeps everything, I mean everything! She's only been teaching ten years and her basement's full of stuff. Do you have more? Lorenzo'll carry it down for you." Lorenzo stood impassive.

They followed Anna up to her apartment. Though Lori had lived downstairs for several years, this was the first time she had been inside. Nor had she spoken much to Anna except to exchange a few polite words when she paid the rent. Since Lorenzo moved in, she seemed to avoid Anna, as if afraid she would disapprove.

"Wow, look at all the books!" Lori breathed.

Anna sat in the rocker, and Lori sat cross-legged on the floor beside her while Lorenzo carried boxes out. "All of them?" he asked. Anna nodded.

Lori said, "Wow!" with a breathy, little-girl sigh.

How strange young people are today, thought Anna. When she was young she wanted to be mature, part of the adult world. Now young people clung to expressions, habits, clothing of immaturity. She began to wonder if the hatred of growing old among old people were not matched or surpassed by the fear, among young people, of growing up.

"We heard you were mugged."

"That's what seems to have happened. I don't know. I can't remember."

"But you weren't hurt?"

Anna shook her head. "Except for this loss of memory. I didn't remember anything at first. Now things are coming back. I was going to look over all those old school things...to give a nudge to my memory, but it...I can't think it would...I don't need...the dust makes me sneeze," she finally declared, knowing it would be impossible to make anyone understand how she felt.

"Imagine," said Lori breathlessly, "to lose your memory. Not to remember anything, like you're new-born, starting all fresh. That must be...what's it like?'' Her interest looked genuine.

Anna shook her head. "Not like being new-born. Because, although I don't remember, it's still all there. Like being in a house suddenly made invisible. Not seeing the walls, one still...bumps into them. And then they're visible...suddenly.'' Anna felt uncomfortable. Maybe she was becoming one of those boring old people who talk to any stranger who will listen, pouring out vague feelings, half-remembered incidents. Lori was looking around the room as if she had something else on her mind.

As Lorenzo came back into the room, he wordlessly handed a few envelopes to Anna. He had picked up the mail. "Thank you,'' Anna said. He stood without moving.

"All done? All gone?'' Lori asked him. He nodded. Then he gave another, shorter nod to Lori, which she returned. It was like a signal. What did it mean? They got up, and Anna followed them to the doorway.

At the door Lori turned to face Anna, cleared her throat and asked, "Have you ever thought of selling this place?''

"No. Well, yes, but not seriously. Don't worry, you'll be able to stay here quite a while yet.''

Lori laughed and shook her head. "I mean we'd like to buy it.''

"Buy it?'' Anna was amazed.

"And restore it. It's such a lovely old house. We'd make it a real house again.''

"And then sell it?''

"Oh, no, live in it! We're thinking about having a baby. So we're going to get married and...''

"That's nice,'' Anna said awkwardly. She had never thought of these two as having any money to buy a house. They were usually late with the small rent she charged.

"...since Lorenzo sold the movie rights on his book, we can go ahead with lots of plans.''

Even more amazed, Anna nodded and looked at Lorenzo. She murmured her congratulations. Evidently this inarticulate man actually had been saving words to put on paper.

"You will think about it!'' begged Lori. "We'd take awfully good care of it, and you'd be free from bothering with it.''

"But then where would I go?''

"Oh, some nice, modern apartment, where you wouldn't have all this to...take care of." To not-take-care-of, to let run down, was the implication, and, Anna thought, quite justified.

"I'll think about it."

After they left, she opened the mail.

One envelope contained her monthly retirement check. The second was a utility bill. There were three advertisements she threw into the waste basket without opening. She opened a blue, square envelope.

It contained a greeting card, covered with pink roses attended by humming birds and edged with shiny gold. The printed message inside was,

> These humming birds have come to say
> Hope you'll soon be well in every way.

Below the printed message was a note, written in pencil, in round, irregular script, the letters pointing in opposite directions, as if about to break loose from the words:

> I saw in the newspaper where you got hurt. I hope you get well real soon. Best of luck from your old puppil, Jake Cabral.

Anna had no idea who Jake Cabral was. She had had many Cabrals and Sanchezes and Williams and Martinis. Anyway, he must have been a student who remembered her fondly, who felt close to her...and who had learned very little English from her. He had probably been, not only a poor student, but a disorderly one. They were the ones who came back to visit their old teachers, who sent them Christmas cards, who were most sentimental about their school days.

She began to smile and then to laugh silently. She did not even know him, had never really known him, though he must have sat in her classroom every day for at least several months. He was a stranger with, no doubt, a good heart. She was laughing at the joke played on her. Here was her reward, here was the message of respect and love, coming across the years, to make all her struggles worthwhile. This was the material from which the conclusion to all those sentimental old movies was made: teacher sighs, sees vision of past students, smiles with fulfillment, fade-out. Her laugh turned hoarse, then abruptly stopped.

The last envelope carried the Board of Education stamp. She

69

expected some routine communication about retirement funds. But it was a real letter.

Dear Miss Giardino:

I wish to convey the extreme concern we all feel at hearing of your unfortunate accident. I was most certainly grateful to learn that your injuries were not serious and that you will soon be your wonderful old self again.

As you may have become aware, there is considerable interest on the part of some newspapers, and much wild speculation, some of which could conceivably reflect on the administration of Camino Real High School, and even on the District as a whole. I am sure that your loyalty to both, and to the good old Mission District, which was once home to me too, will dictate caution in dealing with extreme statements in the media.

To forestall any damaging exaggeration, I know you will want to discourage reporters who might intrude upon you.

I am happy to have this opportunity to send best wishes for a speedy recovery and many happy years to come, to my favorite teacher.

Very truly yours,

Willie
William Fortuna, Director
Disaster Coordination

WF/cb

Anna could feel her heart pounding as her eyes skipped down to the signature, then back to read the letter. Willie Fortuna. It was exactly the kind of letter he would write, pretentious, stupid and overstepping his authority. A letter which warns against doing or saying something that might violate some mythical policy or other, a letter of generalized caution against some non-existent danger, a silly waste of some overworked secretary's time.

Willie Fortuna. Of all things that haunted her teaching years, of all memories she would be glad to forget, Willie was the foremost. How much energy had she wasted hating Willie Fortuna? How many times had she been thwarted by him? Sometimes, she thought that it was not so much the things he did or left undone that hurt her, as it was his continued existence, his success, his standing, serene and unassailable over everything, his absolutely assured place in the center of things, that almost broke her spirit.

What was his title? Good, he was still Director of Disaster Coordination, and he could not be too far from retirement by now. Perhaps, if everyone were lucky, he would stay in that meaningless position, doing no more damage than collecting his high salary. She hoped he would not do another stupid or dishonest thing; if he did, he might, as usual, be promoted out of the job he failed at, to an even higher one, where he. . .*sprawls in his seat, beefy and hungry-looking, frightened, yet sure of himself, defiant and defeated and vain, a classic: the football star without a brain in his thick head. But I don't believe in that label. Everyone has a brain. I'm tired of the jokes about him, tired of the mixture of condescension and affection every time a teacher says his name: Willie Fortuna. In my class he will do the same work as the others, more if he can. I treat him the same as the others. I surprise him. He looks confused, as if wondering if no one has ever told me who he is. As if I have failed to live up to simple expectations, but will eventually come around.*

"Willie, you copied this essay out of a book, this book." I hold up a popular anthology from the library.

"Gee, Miss Giardino, didn't I do what you wanted? Oh. Well, can I make it up?"

"I do not allow make-up on plagiarized papers."

"Plag. . .I don't understand those big words. What does that mean?"

"It means you got an F on that."

Sometimes he turns in nothing at all. "I didn't know how to do it, Miss. G."

"Stay after school and I'll help you."

"And miss football practice!" The whole class laughs. He expects me to fall into the accommodation that all the other teachers have made: Willie must have a C in order that he play football. Give him a C and he will smile cheerfully and make no trouble.

Insist that he earn the C, and there will be trouble.

He comes to class late, and when I send him out, he returns noisily, throwing a pass signed by the coach onto my desk. He mutters under his breath. I turn my eyes on him, and no one dares to giggle, but the threat of distraction is always there. Staring him to silence takes energy. He sighs. He shifts his sprawl. He pretends to fall asleep.

"If this goes on, Willie, you will fail this class."

"Gee, honest? I didn't mean anything, Miss G. I'll try to do better,

honest!"

He begins to turn in his homework. His papers are typewritten, and Willie does not know how to type. They make references to books he cannot have read, using words he has never used. I could waste hours tracking down this more subtle plagiarism, but I refuse to take these hours away from my other students. Besides, he probably does not copy, does not do these papers at all. He has acquired a girlfriend, Rose, a bright, plain girl in the class that meets just after his. I want to take her aside, want to tell her, don't sell out now, not for the sake of a sly brute like Willie. When you leave here, he will be nothing, and you can go on to. . . but I say nothing. Rose and I look at each other, and each of us knows that she does his work for him. She has already made a terrible choice, a choice nearly all the girls make, thinking it is only for the moment, not realizing how habits are formed and kept. She looks at me defiantly, then turns away and will not face me again.

Willie grins like a well-nursed, fat baby, and sprawls more insolently. He looks at me, watches me during classes, with a look of defiant stupidity. His look tells me something, something I gradually read and understand: that stupidity is a decision, a moral decision, not an inherent lack measurable on written tests. I look at Willie's face and I see that he has decided not to grow, but instead to use whatever intelligence he has to defeat my efforts to teach him. He has decided to get whatever he can through manipulations, cunning strategy, deceit. Why is it that what I would find so hard, so impossible to do, becomes easy, the easy way out for Willie? Why does he make this decision?

Always, after Willie, I see that look behind the eyes of any student who says, "I can't," the look that says, "I won't." I hold them all responsible for that decision. I work with them patiently, persistently, but I never accept their refusal, never agree that, yes, they must be too stupid to learn. Maybe that is why, in later years, it is the ones who most disliked me who come back to see me. Those who had decided not to learn still knew that I respected their minds as they had not, that I saw their incapacity as a decision, that I had never given up trying to make them reverse that decision.

Then one day Willie goes too far. Perhaps Rose has been too busy to write a paper for him. Perhaps they have quarreled. Willie turns in his term paper, clearly plagiarized, a little known essay by Bertrand Russell. I smile at the irony and mark an F on the paper. Averaged against his other grades, even allowing for the good papers done by Rose, this makes his final grade a D. It is all clearly documented in my

72

grade book: the absences, the unwritten papers, the poor ones, the few
shining good ones, then the term paper, plagiarized, F.

"You can't give me a D!"

"It should be an F, Willie."

"But I won't be able to play football next year!"

"I have nothing to do with that."

His face becomes ugly with desperation. Hostility and fear merge
with contempt and self-righteousness. Astonishingly, he looks at me
with indignation. "You won't get away with this." As if I have
cheated him. His face is so infantile, so inhuman, that I feel a little
sick watching him shuffle out of the room, his head sunk into his thick
shoulders as if he is crouching to spring.

Later that day I am called to the principal's office. Mr. Simpson,
with his flute and his poetic phrases, is gone. The new Camino High
School has a new principal, the first of the Irish to climb up to high
position in the school system, and one of the worst. Why is it that
when the door opens to a new group, the first to shoot through are
these aggressive opportunists? Mr. O'Day makes the ineffectual old
Mr. Simpson seem like an angel. Mr. O'Day was a baseball coach,
then a counselor, then vice-principal, and is now principal. One rem-
nant of his coaching days remains: a whistle hangs from a dingy string
around his neck, flopping against his striped tie. He often walks down
the halls with a stiff, military posture, blowing his whistle as he sees
behavior he disapproves of, blowing his whistle to summon a teacher
or a student.

"I hear that Willie Fortuna has turned in some unsatisfactory
work." He sits stiffly behind his large desk as if to keep it safely
between us.

I smile. "No, it was very good work, one of Bertrand Russell's
best." Mr. O'Day does not return my smile. "I gave him an F, for
cheating. That's school policy, isn't it?"

"Yes, but..."

"And it wasn't the first time. I warned him before."

Mr. O'Day clears his throat. "Well, yes, but you'll allow him to
make it up?"

"Make it up? Make-up work is allowed for people who are sick
or...I don't allow make-up for a refusal to do the work. When I was
a student here, to be caught cheating was grounds for expulsion. I
think it still is."

"Well, yes, technically. But we try to temper justice with mercy,

73

don't we?"

I say nothing. I remember when this man was baseball coach. how ruthlessly he weeded out players who were less strong and well-coordinated than the leaders, the natural athletes who could win games. And his grading was as ruthless. No matter how hard a boy tried, he got no better than a C if he could not make the team. Sometimes Mr. O'Day's C was the only C on a straight A report card, while a B, above average, has always been possible in my class, for the average student who works hard.

"Do you realize that if Willie doesn't maintain a C average he can't play football next year? All his other grades are C."

"I'm sure they are."

His face turns red, then shifty, almost like Willie's. "I'm surprised at you, Miss Giardino. I thought that you, of all people would want to see Willie make good."

"Make good? Of course, that's what I'm insisting he..." What is he getting at? "What do you mean, me of all people?"

"Well, Willie is one of our Italian boys who could go far... could be an outstanding representative of your people and..."

I just sit as he goes on and on. I am not even insulted by his assumption that I would favor Italians. It's his definition of going far that infuriates me.

"...and you could ruin his future."

"His future?"

"Willie has already attracted attention. If he goes on playing next year he is sure to get a scholarship to a university. Willie is a poor boy..."

"Most of our boys and girls are poor, and some of them should go to college. But I can't see any reason why Willie should. He hates to study, refuses to read. He doesn't belong in college."

"I think your judgment is too hasty. When a student's welfare, perhaps his whole life, is at stake..."

I stand up. "Yes, that's just what is at stake, Willie's welfare. Letting him get away with this. Letting him coast along on his football playing and cheat on everything else. Helping him go to college to continue this lie. It seems to me that all these things are the very worst we could do to Willie. We've already almost ruined him, by not insisting that he use his mind, by not..."

"Miss Giardino, not all people are as academically gifted as you. Willie can't..."

"He can. He can learn to read and write and think to the best of his ability or he can . . . what are we teaching him if we let him get away with this?"

The silence lasts for a full minute. The whistle quivers slightly on his chest. He sighs deeply as if reaching a sad but inevitable conclusion. There is a threat in that sigh. There is a threat in his voice, as he tells me, "Sit down, Miss Giardino," as he reaches toward a manila folder that has been sitting, waiting, near his right hand. "I see you have been with us nearly three years. This is your tenure year."

It is my folder he picks up, mine, yet secret from me, containing my transcripts, assessments of my work, the sheaf of secrets all-powerfully for or against me, following me all my life, throughout my teaching career, determining whether or not I am even to have a teaching career. All this he holds in his hands, idly flipping pages. I look at the folder, then at his face. I do not try to keep the disgust from my eyes. But he does not see it. He is not looking at me. He does not dare to look squarely at me. He is like Willie. He has enough courage to do what he is doing, but just enough for that. Not enough to face me while he does it. He does not have to say more. He does not have to remind me that we are in the depths of the greatest depression this country has known, that it is common for teachers to be fired after a year or two, before getting tenure and higher salary. He does not have to remind me that I have a sick mother to support. On $1600 a year we barely survive. But we survive, as many others do not.

"Are you ordering me to change the grade?"

"No, no. Certainly not. I never tell a teacher what to do in . . . in that respect." He is smiling cheerfully now. He has done this shameful thing, and it is over, like swallowing bad medicine that sours and twists in his mouth, but it is over, except for the sick feeling as it trickles down inside him. Or does he feel that at all? Perhaps he has grown used to the filthy taste of doing things like this.

"Then what are you telling me to do?" I want to make him say it, put it out naked between us and make him look at it.

He puts the folder down. "Just think about it, Miss. G. I'm sure you'll come up with the solution. Think about it."

Think about it. If I were alone there would be nothing to think about. But there is Mama. And she needs her first operation. Since Papa died, she has grown so weak, as if all the weight of her years of strain and overwork and unhappiness has fallen upon her. I could find another job. But where? Most of the offices and stores on Mission

Street have closed, like Stern's Drygoods. Half the houses in The Mission are empty, as people double up in the other half.

I talk to Mama, but she does not understand. She speaks only of how she prays for our neighbors, compared to whom we are now rich. She smiles proudly, secure in her faith that we will never be poor again.

I try David, who only says, "I know what I would do, but I'm weak, I'm not you." And David can offer no other help. His father's business is wiped out, and his mother has made her first suicide attempt. David has yet to earn his first dollar, and has no idea how he or anyone else could.

I try Maggie, the sewing teacher, who says I am too rigid, making too much of a small thing. Then she talks about getting married next month. She has already turned in her resignation, with great relief. Teaching is not her work; it has been only a job, something done cheerfully and efficiently while waiting for marriage.

And Arno cannot focus his attention on such insignificant issues. He talks only about fascism and, pushing aside my petty concerns, borrows money from me to go to Spain. (He gets as far as Baltimore, where he marries the woman in charge of fund-raising for Spanish refugees.)

In the end I cannot give in. Feeling, not courageous or defiant, only tired and stupid and uncertain and alone, like a stubborn child, I refuse to budge.

Nothing happens. I am not fired. I write the D on Willie's report card, but on his official transcript a C appears by magic. I say nothing. The principal says nothing. He never speaks to me again, when he can avoid it. So I have an unexpected reward: I am never again summoned in the hallway by his whistle.

During his senior year Willie's classwork is even worse. I hear it from his teachers, for, of course, he does not take my class again. Even the football coach tells me Willie is a disappointment, and wonders if I, "being Italian and all that," could speak to the boy, about his drinking, his late hours. I tell the coach that I do not think I am the person to do it. Willie's drinking gets worse, but football season ends while Willie still looks good, good enough to get a scholarship to a college with a reputation for little except its football team. Of course, all his teachers give him respectable grades so as not to endanger his scholarship.

On graduation night Willie is missing from the stage when his name is called to receive his diploma. He is in the men's room, vomiting cheap whiskey. I see him lurch out into the hall, pale and shaking, with a trace of vomit streaked across his chin. He stops and looks at me, his face, for once, full of honest shame. Pale and sick and ashamed, he comes as close as he ever has to looking human. I feel as ashamed as he does. I am ashamed for the school, for the way he has been allowed to drift and cheat his way through the past four years. But now will come trials that he is unprepared to meet. He will fail, and his failure will be our fault, our failure. I pity him for the pain I believe must come to him now.

But I am wrong. I could not be more wrong. Willie sails through college with football scholarships that pay him more than some men earn to support a family. He and Rose marry while he is in college, and no doubt she continues to do his schoolwork.

Five years later, Willie is football coach at Camino High School.

In his second year of coaching, Willie is the center of a scandal. His boys are caught with metal plates taped to their arms, illegal armour, an almost lethal weapon. They say Coach Fortuna has supplied them with these devices and told them to say nothing. Willie, interviewed in the daily paper, says he forgot the arm bands are illegal. The athletic association votes to suspend him from coaching for two years. Willie is given a desk in the counseling office.

When the two years are up, Willie stays in counseling. But then comes another incident. One of his duties is allocating scholarship funds, a small amount of money coming from the PTA and alumni association. All the funds, for three years, have gone to cousins of Willie or of his wife. Willie is quietly removed from the counseling office and given the title of Curriculum Consultant. I never figure out exactly what he does in this position. I almost never see him, and when he appears in the teachers' lunchroom on rare occasions, I hear him talking about the boat he is building.

By now we have entered World War II. Most of the men are gone, but Willie is exempted from military service because of an old football injury. When the boys' dean joins the Air Force, Willie takes his place. And as the war ends, Principal O'Day hangs up his whistle and retires, and Willie Fortuna becomes principal of Camino Real. He keeps this position for a record ten years. How? Perhaps he has learned, at least, to do nothing so blatant as to cause his removal, to do nothing, nothing at all.

Our first race riot explodes on a day when Willie is on one of his

77

frequent trips to Tahoe. No one can tell exactly what led to the riot. What led to it is everything, everything. The school is simply lost in an avalanche of neglect, of new problems piled onto the old ones. Everything has deteriorated, the building, supplies, teaching, attendance, discipline, even the football team. We have had all the problems of the war and post-war changes dumped upon us, with no one to oversee the search for solutions but Willie Fortuna.

Instantly the superintendent removes Willie, replacing him with another man (and another and another, all of whom seem hardly different from Willie). And what will happen to Willie? The only logical answer is further promotion, to the central office, where Willie is put in charge of the supply department.

The Department of Budget and Supply has always been hopeless. Principals must send in long, detailed lists of supplies for approval or order by central administrators. The backlog of work is so bad that lists must be submitted over a year ahead. Schools order more than they need, to be sure of having enough, and cannot anticipate some needs so far ahead. The result is that the school is full of useless, deteriorating materials, while we lack the things we need.

Willie's reign cannot make things worse, and no one expects it ever to get better. He could go on forever in Supply.

But no. Irregularities are noticed, strange gaps in the inventory lists, extreme even for the chaotic Supply Department. There are rumors that Willie has been selling school supplies. Nothing is said officially, nothing is even hinted, but Willie is again quietly removed from this job and promoted to a higher one.

When I hear his new title I laugh and laugh. Director of Disaster Coordination. Now he has no access to either people or money. His only function, it seems, is to allot a certain number of AIR RAID SHELTER signs to be uselessly posted over basement entrances to schools. Since tensions with Russia have already eased by this time, and everyone is forgetting the insane plans to go underground or attempt mass evacuations during atomic bombing, it is a fairly safe, sure assumption that Willie Fortuna is simply sitting at the downtown office, doing nothing.

Anna looked down at her hands. The letter was crumpled, torn, twisted, almost shredded. She got up and threw the pieces into the fireplace. But, as she did, she wondered if even now Willie had lost the capacity to do more than anger an old woman. She half-believed that he would yet manage to do something bad enough to force the school board to remove him from his present position. And, in that case, there would be no place to put him but at the top, as superintendent.

She leaned against the mantelpiece, another sudden wave of fatigue washing over her. She closed her eyes for a moment but only felt more unsteady, dizzy. She opened them, shook her head and went to the bedroom. She would have to lie down for a few minutes until her weakness passed. She curled up on the bed, on her side, and was instantly asleep.

She jolted awake, pulled back too suddenly from deep sleep, confused, not sure where she was or what time it was. The phone shrieked in her ear. It was attached in her study, but a long cord allowed it to be placed near her bed, where it sat now, ringing and ringing. She picked it up.

"Miss Giardino?"

"Yes."

"This is Maria Flores. I was a student of yours at Camino. I graduated in 1960. I don't know if you remember me."

"Maria. Yes," Anna lied. Flores's came by the dozens. But she was not really lying. She would remember Maria after they talked for a while. She always did, with a little time, a little talk, remember a student. "How are you?" Maria's voice would tell her; soon she would recognize it. Voices were often a deeper, clearer expression of identity than faces. But why hadn't she just admitted she didn't remember the girl? She was getting defensive about her memory loss.

"I read about you in the newspaper. You were mugged."

"It seems likely."

"You weren't seriously hurt, the paper said."

"No, I'll be fine, thank you."

There was a pause. Anna waited for whatever it was the girl had to say, and Maria seemed to be hesitating as if she did not know how to say it.

"I'd like to visit you."

"That would be very kind," said Anna, thinking that it would be awkward if their visit were comprised of a limping conversation like this one.

"Not to be kind," said Maria, as if it were important to be strictly, literally truthful. "I mean...there are some things I've wanted to say...ever since...there's unfinished business between us."

Anna could not think what to answer.

79

"Could I come tomorrow afternoon?"

"All right. I live at..."

"I know where you live." Anna heard a giggle, the first sign of the girl's relaxing a bit, the first vaguely familiar sound from her. "We all knew where you lived. We used to watch you walking up that hill after school. Stanley Cooper used to say he could feel you watching him from up there. Do you remember Stanley, tall black boy, always wore a red cap?"

"Yes, of course, Stanley." Anna was pleased that she remembered him well. A bright, hard-working boy. She had gotten him a scholarship to...what college?

"He was killed in Vietnam, you know."

"No, I didn't."

After Anna hung up the phone she lay back again, falling into a weary stupor, not quite asleep, awake enough to feel her body relaxing, to feel the awful aching tiredness evaporate slowly. This was more satisfying, almost, than deep sleep, this suspended, painless state in which she could enjoy being conscious of her comfort.

Thump! Thump! Just below, right under her bed, the signal called her. *Mama needs me!* She opened her eyes. No, not Mama. Mama was dead, had been dead for years. She used to poke at the ceiling with a broom until she was too weak for that and Anna began sleeping on a cot next to her bed. No, it was Arno. How funny that Arno imitated her mother's habit, rapping on the ceiling with a broom handle when he wanted her. He hardly ever came up to her apartment, but always summoned her to his when he needed something or when he was in one of his fierce depressions. (He did not retire from the world as David's mother had done, but demanded an audience for his bitter speeches on the world's present state of deterioration.)

She was too tired. It was her turn to be sick and depressed. Arno would have to wait. She closed her eyes.

But he would not relent. The thumping began again, harder, sharper and more insistent. She was afraid he would break the plaster. She got up and dragged herself out to the top of the stairway to call him and tell him that she was too tired to do anything for him.

"Damn it, Anna, come down here before dinner gets completely cold!"

He had made an omelette for her, and a small fruit salad. He was an excellent cook of simple things like this, and served the food attractively if haphazardly on one of the small tables, using two of the lavender napkins which Anna's mother had crocheted.

He did not eat at all, only watched as Anna, suddenly realizing how hungry she was, ate quickly and with pleasure.

"There," he said, when she finished.

"Thank you. I feel much better now."

He nodded. "Now go on up to bed."

"Yes, I'd better get some sleep. I'm having a visitor tomorrow, and I can't think who she is."

That night her fire dream included a faceless young girl who Anna knew was Maria Flores. She was caught in the inner court just outside the girls' gym. There were sheer walls on all sides of her and fire all around her. Anna could see her from a window above which looked down on the court. She let down a rope and called to Maria to grab it.

Then she began to pull her up. But the rope began to swing with Maria like a great weight, like a silent bell, hanging from the end, swinging back and forth in wide sweeps, almost touching the walls on all sides of the court. The rope began to slip through Anna's fingers. "Oh, God there must be a knot at the end." But there was no knot. The rope slipped through her burning palms and Maria fell. She lay crushed and bloody but conscious. She looked up at Anna with hurt, accusing eyes, and now Anna saw her face clearly and knew her.

Anna shook her head. "I didn't mean to. . ." She heard someone giggling beside her. It was Miss Patterson, the art teacher who always kept a bottle of gin in her desk. She grinned as she stood beside Anna, holding her bottle of gin, which sprouted flames.

"Well, I'm not surprised." She blew out the flames like a candle and took a deep gulp from the bottle. "She was like you, that was the trouble. She had a chance to get out, but you didn't want her to get away."

"Liar!" Anna yelled. "You always lied. You lied then. You're lying now. Liar!"

But the woman only smiled as Anna felt hotter and hotter. The flames were getting closer.

"Hold my hand," said Miss Patterson, "and I'll teach you to fly. We'll forget about her."

But Anna pulled back from her touch.

"Suit yourself," said Miss Patterson gaily, as she rose up and out through the open window. She hovered there for a moment, smiling drunkenly, then floated away.

THURSDAY

WHEN ANNA WOKE, she lay in bed for a long time, her eyes roving the ceiling, then down the walls along the rows of books. Usually she got right up, got moving, before she could think too much about the early morning stiffness, the aches that would vanish after an hour of activity. But she had awakened remembering who Maria was. Each time the girl came into her mind, she squirmed with shame. She felt the shame, it seemed, in every joint, along with her usual pain.

She heard sounds from below. Arno was up. She put on a pair of pants and a sweater, and went downstairs.

As soon as he opened the door, he squinted at her and cocked his head slightly. "What's up?"

"I just wanted to talk."

"Right." Arno looked pleased. "Tea's ready."

Anna shook her head.

Carrying his cup, Arno sat down on the sofa, spilling a few more drops on it. He sat silently waiting until Anna began.

"There's a student, a Mexican girl called Maria Flores, coming to see me this afternoon. When she called, I couldn't remember who she was. But now I remember." Anna sat down on the edge of the sofa, then got up again. "Yesterday you and I talked about students hating teachers, with or without reason. She is one who has reason to hate me."

"You mean she had something to do with the attack on you?"

"Oh, no, not that." Anna stood near the window. "I haven't thought of her, not since she graduated. I didn't want to."

Arno waited.

"It was just before Mama died. She hardly got up anymore. I slept on a cot next to her. It was the year we had three riots, aside from the usual scuffles." Anna realized she was putting off telling, and making excuses for what she would finally tell. "I knew Maria before I ever had her in a class. Teachers talk. They complain about most of the

82

students, but they praise the good ones too. In a school like Camino, they overpraise the good ones.

"Maria was bright. Maria read avidly. Maria was respectful and polite. Maria was clean. Maria was pretty. Maria did not drink. Maria was on time every day. Maria worked part time to support her eight brothers and sisters. Maria wrote brilliantly. Maria was not like those other Mexicans. That infuriated me. It made me remember: 'Anna is not like those other Italians.'

"I first saw her when a teacher pointed her out in the hall. She was tall for a Mexican and quite dark. Her body was very mature and developed, like most of the Mission girls. (Why do poor people mature sexually before people with money and security? Is it just that they get old faster?) Her body was a bit heavy, but her face was delicate and bright. There was a kind of steady, serious look in her eyes.

"She finally ended up in my Senior English class, as all college-bound students did. She had been patted and petted and praised for years. Then she got her first C, from me, on the first paper she turned in. She was furious, insulted. She had never been told that anything she did was less than marvelous. She was lazy. She had no idea how lazy she was. She had no idea what real work was.

"Of course, I let students rewrite papers for a better grade. She rewrote...and rewrote. She sat grim-faced, staring at me with those steady eyes, so angry and hurt. The other students noticed. They had always been cool toward her, envious. Now they were sympathetic, almost friendly. Her papers were better than theirs, yet more covered with red marks. Of course. In the better papers I had more to work on. She wrote one paper on teacher prejudice against Chicanos. After four rewrites she abandoned it. It had been an accusation of me, you see, and she knew it was false.

"We struggled on until one day she turned in quite a good paper. When she got it back with an A on it, she knew she deserved it, she knew what a good paper was. She gritted her teeth while she gave me a tiny smile. Then she started coming in early in the morning, when she knew I would be alone in my room, asking me for advice on papers she did for other classes, on writing she did just for herself. What it came to by the end of that year was something almost like the feeling I'd had with students years before, even with whole classes. The way it used to be. On my terms. No easy, false familiarity. We were very formal. Certainly we couldn't be friendly. The other students might notice, and then they wouldn't be able to forgive her for her brilliance. They wouldn't like her any more, as they'd started to do since old Miss Giardino began to persecute her. So we played a game. On the surface, very stiff, but underneath...I believe there was something..."

Now Anna was becoming awkward and slow again. "It was such a bad year for me. Mama's worst times came at night. I hardly got any sleep. All discipline had broken down at school...the halls were like..."

"Yes," Arno interrupted. "I heard about all that. I held your hand during those last years, remember, trying to get you to retire early, instead of hanging on in that stubborn...let's not go through it all again." Arno sat up straight, then leaned forward to rub his knee joints as he grimaced with pain.

"Maria was the only positive thing in my life just then. I felt old and tired. And Maria responded...it was..."

"In other words," said Arno, "you'd been reduced to getting all your satisfaction from one student. A very dangerous position to be in. I almost know what's coming next."

"It was such a stupid thing! Maria turned in her last paper, an indictment of her own lazy habits. The subject was intelligence tests. One of the points Maria made was that even if the concept of the IQ meant something, it was a useless concept because so few people ever used any of this so-called intelligence. Her examples were vivid. Her words were precise, full of conviction. Organization, transitions... excellent. I put an A on the paper and added a note that her improvement warranted an A in the course. I seldom gave an A.

"She said nothing when she looked at the paper, not a word. We kept our rule of silence, kept the roles we played. But I heard her swing out into the hall, chanting, "An A, an A, an A!"

"Next morning in the lounge, I was resting when Elva Patterson came in. Did I ever tell you about her?"

Arno nodded. "The one who took a nip before each class."

"She taught art. That is, she gave assignments, then sat in class reading magazines. That's how she spent thirty years at Camino. No one ever criticized her, or said she injured her students, or that she was prejudiced or..." Anna brought her voice under control. "Elva Patterson smirked at me and said hello, giggling as if she knew of a joke on me. I nodded but didn't speak. I had always despised her, and she knew it and kept away from me. But this time she didn't go away. She stood around smirking, looking into the mirror and patting her hair. Finally she said, 'I guess Maria Flores wins her bet.' I still didn't answer her. 'I mean, you didn't spoil her straight A record after all. She found a way to get around you.'

"I answered something to the effect that she was getting an A from me because she had earned it. I hadn't slept all night. My head was pounding. She giggled and said, 'Oh, yes, she earned it, especially with that subject. I didn't think she could put it over on you, but she did it.' Then I played right into her hands. I asked her what she meant. 'Clever girl. How students don't use their capabilities. Just what you've been saying all these years, like a tape recording of yourself. Comforting, isn't it, to hear your own words, your own opinions parrotcd back at you.'

"She left the room before I could say a word. And then I acted like a fool. If only I hadn't had such a headache, or the noise in the halls were not so deafening, or if only the class Maria was in was not the first period of the day. If I'd had time to think, I would never. . .

"I walked into the classroom. I saw Maria sitting there, laughing at something the boy next to her had said, still laughing as she turned to look at me, as if she were laughing at me, or it seemed so." Anna stopped and put her hand up on the window frame, leaning against it and staring hard at the overgrown bush which obscured the view. "I said, 'Having your little joke?' The class hushed, listening, watching. 'Putting something over on Miss Giardino? Well, that paper is an F, like any dishonest paper. Think about that before you decide to get around Miss Giardino. Make your bets more carefully!' "

Anna did not look at Arno to see his reaction. She was too ashamed, even now, nine years later, too ashamed to want to hear what he thought. When Arno remained silent she went on, to the end, still looking out the window.

"She just sat there. Everyone sat there. No one had ever seen me do anything like that. I never had, never. I assigned a grammar exercise and sat down at my desk, pretending to read papers. I couldn't read or think. After a while I heard Maria get up and leave the room. She never came back. I never reported her absences. I turned in a B grade for her. I never saw her again.

"I knew I was wrong. I knew it while I was accusing her. The girl had worked hard and she really did write well by the end of the semester. How could any words from a malicious old drunk make me do anything so. . .''

"You've already answered that question. You were going through a bad time.''

"That's no excuse, not for a teacher."

"Oh, for God's sake, Anna. People do it all the time. Blow off steam at the nearest poor devil, who then does it to someone else, passing the guff down the line."

"But a teacher must be fair. That's the highest compliment a student pays a teacher...to say, 'she's fair.' No matter what: headaches, or worse. A teacher must be fair."

"Bullshit. No human being is fair all the time."

"A teacher isn't supposed to be human."

"Well, for the love of God," Arno mumbled as he got to his feet, frowning as he flexed his stiff joints. "I thought you were going to tell me about some heinous crime, and you tell me this."

"You have to see it in the context of..."

"I do! And let me suggest something to you. If all you teachers are breaking your backs to be fair, then I'd say you're giving your students damned rotten training to survive in the world, damned bad preparation for life. Life isn't fair, Anna. You can say it's a lot of other things, but it isn't fair."

"No, it isn't." Anna sank down on the sofa, tired but not relieved. Nothing Arno said lessened her sense of shame.

"Now, look, the girl liked you. Respected you. She has probably forgotten all about the incident. She read about you in the paper. I'll make you a bet. She won't even mention that incident. She'll talk about old school days, as if it never happened. If she's half the girl you say she is..."

"You're probably right." Anna stood up. "What other reason could she have..."

Arno put his arms around her. Arno's moments of tenderness always came as a surprise, as if he were incapable of showing affection and care unless he could take her unawares. "Like me," he said. "When I came back to you, I never mentioned or remembered what we'd quarreled about the last time we were together."

Anna did not answer. Her mind was skipping, like a pebble thrown across a pool: Arno's reappearance in 1930 when the depression forced him back from Paris; Arno during the war, when he resolved to leave his wife and demanded Anna marry him; Arno in 1953 when he lost his radio job because of his socialist connections; and finally Arno in 1965, divorced and ill. This, his last stay, had been his longest, their longest time together, though now, of course, they were no longer together.

It was she who had never mentioned his most recent desertion each time he returned, needing her, taking it for granted that she would be there, that she was too intelligent (as he put it) to be petty, too generous to hold a grudge, too decent to rake up old injuries and throw them at him when he was down. She suppressed a smile and let herself be comforted in his arms, though she knew from experience that this was not a very secure place to be. But the old, she thought, learn to take momentary comforts wherever they find them.

"Now," said Arno, abruptly dropping his arms. "Get yourself up like the proper model of a favorite teacher, and relax. That mugging did one thing for you. It's putting you in touch with people again, reminding them you're alive. You'll have more visits from others who saw the newspaper article. And a good thing too. I've hardly seen you speak to a soul lately, except for that old witch across the street."

What old witch? Anna's memory had failed her again. But she did not worry about it. She was beginning to believe in the eventual recovery of everything she wanted to remember. Even the attack itself. With the thought of it came the now familiar chill, the sense of dread. What on earth could she so dread remembering?

She went upstairs, showered and dressed herself in an old gray skirt and sweater that she had worn continually during her last ten years of teaching. The clothes of the old never wear out, she thought. But she felt better. Telling Arno about the old incident had reduced it to its proper size.

She ate. She tried to read, sitting by the window, but could not concentrate, could not sit still. She began to clean up the apartment, dusting haphazardly and putting things in order. Most of her life she found housework a silly, boring chore, to be gotten rid of quickly. But now she enjoyed moving about slowly, creating order, though each time she put something away, she felt she should fill more boxes with things to be carried down to the garbage by Lorenzo.

Then the bell was ringing, the door opening, and Maria faced her. "I wondered what you'd look like, how much you'd changed. But you look exactly the same, even your clothes."

Anna nodded. "You've changed."

Maria was thinner. She wore pants and a sweater, and her long black hair was pulled back severely. Her skin was darker than ever, as if she spent much time in the sun, and she looked, not Mexican, but rather oriental. They sat down near the window, Anna in the rocking chair and Maria on the footstool which she insisted was quite comfortable.

After a long silence, Anna began guardedly, "And what have you been doing these past . . . eight or nine years, isn't it?"

Maria looked surprised. "I'm at Camino. Didn't you know?"

Anna stiffened. "I've lost touch since I retired. So you did go to college."

"College, marriage, motherhood, divorce . . ." Maria smiled tightly as if listing disasters. "I replaced you at Camino." Her voice was ironic, but her eyes looked merely tired.

"So this would be your fourth year." When Maria nodded, Anna asked, "But is today a holiday?"

Maria shook her head and flushed. "I took a day of sick leave. I guess you would disapprove. Someone told me you never took a day off in forty years."

"Not at all," said Anna. "When my mother died, and . . . some other times." She could not remember any other times. A long silence followed, as if both were waiting for her to remember. "Is Stewart Warner still head of the English Department?"

"Oh, yes. He hasn't changed. He's very nice."

"Yes, I'm sure he is that!" Anna was surprised by her own voice. Bitter, sarcastic, slipping into anger again.

But Maria only smiled. "I'd almost forgotten. You two didn't get on very well, did you?"

"Who told you that?"

Maria shrugged. "Students know."

"We had different philosophies . . . different approaches," Anna said cautiously, since she felt so near to blurting out furious feelings. "I suppose there's room for many different styles of teaching." She did not believe that. In his gentle, smiling way, Stewart Warner had done much to undermine her, to let the students think they were right to resent her formal manner, her strict demands upon them. She felt the old arguments between her and Stewart coming back into her memory. She did not want to live through all of them again. "Why have you come?" she asked bluntly. "What can I do for you?"

Maria hesitated. "Well, I saw the newspaper article, and I thought, there's Miss Giardino still up the hill, close by me every day, and I've never gone to see her, so I thought I'd just . . . drop in and see what you're doing now that you're retired. You must have lots of time to . . . to do . . . lots of things . . ."

Anna shrugged. "Like what?"

"I always thought you'd write a book."

"Book? What sort of book?"

"Well, you taught at Camino for forty years, and went to school there too, didn't you? Stewart and I were just saying the other day, that you must have known the place for fifty years!"

Anna nodded.

"There! Why, a book on the ethnic waves alone . . ."

"Ethnic waves?" Oh, yes. Soul. La Raza. Finding cultural roots that had no individual reality, but supplied instant identity, simple answers to questions that took a lifetime to answer. Perhaps this girl was writing a book herself, and wanted information. That explained her visit.

Anna relaxed a bit and nodded. "Waves of the poor. When I was a student at Camino, the old, established people were northern European, Scandinavian, vanishing from The Mission. I was part of the next wave: Italian, Irish, Russian. The teachers used to complain about the noisy Italian boys. They said the old Swedish boys were fine, but these Italians . . ." Anna laughed. "I was different, of course; they assured me I was different."

"Me too," said Maria, "Not like 'those other Mexicans.' "

"In the thirties, when I was starting to teach, the Irish and Italians and Russians were the 'good' ones, and the next wave were poor whites coming in from the dust bowl. Thin, pale children with tight skulls. Pasty faces; even their freckles were unattractive, made their skins look more sickly white. They were bitter and sullen, rather than noisy. They were always picking fights with the Italian boys and losing because they were so thin."

"What happened to them?"

Anna shrugged. "A few years of decent food, and they moved out of The Mission, over Twin Peaks or down The Peninsula."

"And then came the Latinos," Maria murmured.

Anna nodded. "There were always some Mexicans, but these were different, coming just after the war started. Pachucos. It was their word. Gangs. The girls wore their hair in high pompadors, sometimes with knives tucked into them. The boys wore zootsuits. Do you know what a zootsuit is?" Maria shook her head. Anna did not think it was important to describe the zootsuits. "The pachuco gangs fought with sailors. At school they fought with knives. We'd always had fights between the old and the new students, but never with knives before."

Anna watched for signs that Maria was offended, but she saw only interest and curiosity. "I almost left teaching then. The war opened new jobs. Everyone was leaving."

"Why didn't you?"

"And leave the students to every incompetent misfit the school board grabbed! No, someone had to stay."

"What happened to the pachucos?" asked Maria.

Anna laughed. "The pachuco boys married the pachuco girls and became the strictest parents in The Mission."

"My parents?" said Maria. "They'd never admit it." She laughed and hugged her legs, resting her chin on her knees. "And then who...the Blacks were next, I guess," she prodded.

Anna nodded. "All over again. Poor, and badly fed...the same problems, only worse, of course." Why was it so much worse, so much harder? Well, Anna thought, I was older and tired. Tougher problems and fewer resources to deal with them. And something more. Less faith that I could, that I held the answers. Perhaps Anna could write a book. The history of her years at Camino would be a history of the city, perhaps, in some ways, she thought, of the whole nation. It was an interesting idea, but one to tuck away, not to discuss now. "Tell me about your teaching. What's the new wave?"

Maria shrugged. "More Latinos, always more, and Blacks and Filipinos, and . . . but the biggest wave hitting The Mission now is gay, and they don't have children, so . . . maybe there won't be any more waves of the poor."

Anna shook her head and quoted, "The poor you always have with you . . ."

"If they can still afford the rents in The Mission!"

"They'll just double up . . . the way they did during The Depression, and then . . ."

"You know what I really came here for," blurted Maria, as if afraid that if she did not say it quickly she would not say it at all.

"I can't imagine," said Anna.

"To ask you some questions, important questions. To tell you some things. To apologize."

"Apologize?"

"You've probably forgotten all about it . . ."

"No, I haven't forgotten." So Arno was wrong. The subject finally had come up. "Apologize? Then you did concoct a paper that would appeal to my prejudices, to win your bet, to . . ."

"No! I worked harder in your class than I ever knew I could . . .

and I meant every word of that paper."

"Then it is I who owe you the apology," said Anna, feeling herself go rigid.

Maria shrugged. "I was so self-righteous. I hated you. I hated you for a long time. You were the nasty old teacher who'd been unfair to me. Me! I was so important, to me. When I was hired to replace you at Camino, I felt vindicated. It was symbolic. I was the New Teacher: free, lively, pretty . . ." Maria blushed, smiled and shook her head. Some of her hair had come loose. She did look very pretty, especially with her expression of good-humored self-criticism. "Until a little while ago. I'm not sure just when, but I started thinking about you. The more I taught, the more I remembered you. This past year especially. I realized I owe you an apology. For judging you. Because I understand." Maria laughed, but her laugh was not pretty. "Only three years of teaching, and do I understand!"

Anna leaned back in the chair, listening, trying to understand whatever it was the girl was telling her.

"I didn't when I started. I just wanted to be popular. I wanted them to love me. For the first two years, I just wanted everyone to . . . and I succeeded, only, of course, I wasn't real. That's what it is like, being a popular young teacher. Always proving how young you are, proud of being mistaken for a student by the other teachers." Maria's face had twisted as if she smelled something bad. "I wasn't myself. Every move, every gesture, wasn't really me."

"Do you think I was myself?" asked Anna.

"No, but at least you didn't take the easy way out. You acted the strict authoritarian, to make us work and study and learn. I've acted out their teenage girlfriend fantasies." She made a disgusted sound in her throat, then took a deep breath. "Then last year I clamped down. We were going to have order and quiet . . . and learn."

"What happened?"

"I was called a traitor to Third World people. Cruel, too demanding. In one class, the best one, I tried to have it out with them, tried to talk about what they were studying and whether they objected to learning it, why they were resisting. I couldn't get them to talk about anything but whether or not they *liked* me. Finally I said, 'But what does it matter to you whether or not you like me? Don't think of me, think of yourselves. What you can learn from me is what matters, not whether or not you like me.' They just didn't understand what I was saying." Maria sighed. "This year, I started out a little better, not a

91

drill sergeant, not their girlfriend . . . somewhere between, I hoped: firm, demanding, but fair.''

''And how is it this year?''

Maria bit her lip. "Even harder! But better. I mean, I knew I was doing better for them. But then, last week, something happened . . . those pencils. Those damned pencils. Nobody even brings his own pencil to school; we don't even mention pens anymore. So we issue pencils in class. And there's a short supply, something got fouled up on last year's requisition. So they're rationed. Slips to fill out, delays, fights with the supply clerk . . . anyway, it was after lunch, my toughest class, you know how hard it is to settle them down after lunch. I opened my drawer, and they were gone, the whole box. Someone had stolen the pencils. A prank by a student, maybe. Or a teacher might have run out, and rather than go through all that red tape . . . anyway, they were gone.

''Just a stupid little thing, not a tragedy, not a subject worth talking about, not even an interesting story. Boring. Happens every day. Boring things like that. Yes, that's it, every day for months and years. Little petty things just like that.

''I started to shake. I just stood there shaking and thinking, is this what I became a teacher for? I start to shake again just thinking about it. You understand, don't you?''

Anna nodded.

''And I thought, it doesn't matter what plans I make or how hard I work. What happens in my classroom will be determined by petty little foul-ups like this, a thousand of them, routine, built into the system and happening so regularly they aren't even worth talking about. Do you know what I mean?''

Anna nodded again.

''Just. . .just wearing me down. Nothing I can do about them. I don't know. If I go on this way, I'll end up like Miss Patterson, with a bottle in her desk, or like that football coach, what's his name, the one who'd goad the boys till they hurt each other during practice, and then he'd laugh at their bloody faces. But if I just hang on, control my feelings, try to do a job in spite of it . . .'' She stopped, bit her lip, then turned to look out of the window.

''You'll end up like me,'' Anna finished for her. The girl said nothing, kept staring out the window. Yes, there was already a certain tight lift to her jaw. "It's a bad time," said Anna, "the fourth year."

''And the tenth? and the twentieth? and the thirtieth . . .'' Maria's face seemed to search the horizon far across the city. "It does something to you."

"What do you want me to tell you?" Anna asked. "That it doesn't have to be that way? I think you came to the wrong person."

"Then let me ask you one more question," said Maria. "Does it help if I tell you that you were the best teacher I ever had? If I say, in spite of what happened between us, I learned more from you than from anyone else, that I use methods I learned in your class, and they're still good. Does it help, in your feeling about Camino and all those years, when I tell you that?"

Anna smiled and took a deep breath while she thought. "I'd like to say that makes it all worthwhile. But . . ." She shrugged. Did knowing you were in the right help after the car had run over you?

"Then I just can't understand why you didn't leave teaching."

Anna hesitated, almost stammering at such a strange question. "Teaching was my work."

Maria waited as if Anna must have more to say. But what else was there to say? Finally Maria stood. "I have to pick up my son at nursery school."

"I'm glad you came, Maria." Anna stood and extended her hand. Their handshake was firm, as if sealing an agreement. "No matter what I said, it meant a great deal to me, your visit. I'm only sorry that I wasn't able to be of more help, to tell you something useful."

Maria looked steadily into Anna's eyes as she said, "Miss Giardino, I've never spoken to you without learning something. May I come again?"

Anna was surprised. "Why, yes. If you really want to."

"I really want to."

Anna sat down in the rocking chair again. The soft tones of Maria's voice seemed to echo in the room. Anna had missed that sound, the smoothed off, mellow words of her Mexican students. Not an accent, of course, and not like the Italian sound, which blunted the words more. They all had it, even the ones who, like Maria, were born here. A muted, dark softening of the words, warm and moist like the air of Oaxaca after the rain. *"But you've never been to Mexico?"*

I shake my head. "I've never traveled at all, hardly left the Bay Area."

"Oh, but you must go!"

We sit in the teacher's room listening to yet another of them recite

93

her adventures of last Christmas in Mexico City. Now that the war is over, now that we teachers are making enough to live on and a bit more, we fly off into the world during our vacation. It is April, the time of telling summer plans, and everyone is going somewhere: Mexico, Canada, Europe, Japan.

"Where are you going this summer, Miss G.?"

I shrug. "I really hadn't thought of going anywhere."

"I suppose you'll be busy working on your house."

I have owned the Phoenix Street house for nearly a year. The roof is fixed and the garden planted. Mama is happily settled in the first floor apartment.

". . . and, of course, your mother needs you. How is she?"

"Surprisingly well, right now." She could do without me for a while. She has even told me I should get away. Maybe I should take a trip, start with Mexico, as all the others seem to do.

"You would love Mexico! So colorful, so varied, so cheap!"

Yes, I want to go somewhere, want to get away. Maybe what decides me is the letter I have had from Arno, saying that he and his wife will, for the sake of the children, try once more. It is a nasty, whining letter, ending with a fatuous statement of certainty that I, such an intelligent woman, will understand and forgive him.

And so, I suddenly declare over the lunch table, "Yes, I think I'll go to Mexico this summer."

Trains and buses, a short flight and more buses. Just getting there is exhausting, past the awful border towns, through the desert. Traveling is harder than I expected. Only the language is easy. I mix my Italian with the Spanish I have learned from my students, and I do well enough.

But I am learning that I am not a traveler. Not like other people, who get rest and relief, get out of themselves, by moving in space. Perhaps they invent dramas for themselves, to play against a foreign, exotic background. But I cannot. Do I lack imagination? Where are the quaint villages? The colorful people? I see desolate desert encampments and hungry people. This poverty makes my childhood seem a paradise. I feel ashamed to witness such hunger and illness. This is no exotic background for my adventures. It is a real country, inhabited by real people, trying to survive, just as people do at home, but trying in the face of terrible odds. What is wrong with me? Why do I not see what others see? Why can't I relax and enjoy the fact that here, in this place, compared to these people, I am a rich lady, who can demand

94

every service and comfort. I am ashamed, and not sorry that I am ashamed.

If I were an affluent twenty-year-old, these sights might be educational, but I am forty-three. There are some things I already know.

I hurry away from the small villages, toward the cities, where there will be less poverty. And in the cities, just a few blocks from my hotel, I experience a sense of familiarity. What am I reminded of? Of Mission Street, of the new warborn Mission Street, where stores, closed during The Depression, have opened again with huge garish signs, piles of trinkets and poorly made clothes in gaudy colors. Here in Mexico the Indians fingering the cheap jewelry, spending money that should buy food, buying some gaudy substitute for the hope missing from their lives. . . all this reminds me of the Gypsies, Okies, Mexicans and Negroes on Mission Street since the war.

Of course, there is another, an elegant part of the cities, walled suburbs open to those who have friends here. I have none. In the Mission District one does not meet affluent Mexicans who would have relatives in such places. The relatives of my students are starving back in the villages. I walk the streets, from museums to ruins to churches, followed by begging children or by smirking men. I begin to imagine that all around me are hungry, hostile eyes, resenting the indecency of a lone woman, yet hoping to exploit me. Perhaps it is not only my imagination. (So I do have imagination?)

In the hotel bars I see another picture. Women like myself, more elegantly dressed, but no younger, some of them American, clearly teachers or librarians or social workers, all attended by eager, fawning Mexican men. The men all look the same: plump, with black, slicked-down hair and pencil-thin moustaches. They all wear blue serge suits. In this heat. I cannot tell one from the other. I seem to see one man over and over again, ordering a drink, leaning forward to light the cigarette of a middle-aged American lady. Is this what many of those teachers really come here for? All those women, those lonely, single schoolteachers, do they come here, not for the ruins and climate, as they tell me, but for a few weeks of romance by a slightly paunchy imitation of an old Hollywood movie Latin lover?

I see some American women traveling together, looking like teachers, laughing, talking, enjoying each other. I could join such a group. More teachers? Like the ones I left. That is not what I have come here for. What have I come here for? I have no idea. I try to be a conscientious tourist. I take bus tours, plod through churches,

95

museums. I climb the pyramids outside Mexico City.

One day I take the all day bus trip to Oaxaca, and decide to stay. It seems different, an old Spanish town where the poverty seems not so agonizing, and the pace not so frantic as in the cities. There is a university and enough churches and ruins to keep me busy for some days. I stay in the old, thick-walled hotel on the Zocalo. My room is on the ground floor, dark and cool, with long barred and shuttered windows.

When I open the shutters at night, I can watch the people promenading round and round the Zocalo, families walking, children running rings around them, young people flirting with long glances as they hang back from their parents. Lights are strung across the square, and a band plays, its sound reaching me in uneven waves. The air carries a warm, sweet scent. I sit in the window, watching the people and the flickering lights, and finally, if only fleetingly, I feel a release, a letting go, floating free and weightless in a strange, foreign place, and yet. . . and yet in a place that, somewhere inside me, I have always known. I have finally arrived. . . somewhere.

This strange sense of arrival fills me, like the scent in the air. It makes tears come to my eyes. Is it the altitude? I feel as if I have made a sentimental return to some peaceful place I know well. I have come home to something remembered and longed for though never seen before. Lights spread in my tear-filled eyes, like glimmering haloes looking for a head to light upon. I am returning to a place I have never seen, to a childhood I have never known. What kind of memory is this? Do my Italian genes hold something like this scene, or does something Mama has said about her childhood in Italy match this?

I stop asking. I only see and feel it, until the music dies away and the last of the stragglers goes home for the night.

The next morning I eat breakfast on the hotel patio, looking out onto the Zocalo. Like the others sitting at tables around me, I sit for a long time watching the people going about their work, the young people on their way to school. I hear a conversation in English near me, an argument about Hemingway. At the next table they are talking in Spanish, about digs: archeologists working on newly found ruins. There are still the begging children, the men selling blankets or carrying huge trays of fly-covered food for sale. But the people are kindly, unself-conscious, tolerant of one another.

No one takes any notice of me as I get up. No one follows me and smirks at me. Once off the Zocalo I am among walled Spanish houses. A few minutes walk and I am on the edge of the town, facing a broad plain and valleys below, mountains beyond. The silence is soothing. But my own silence is tiring. I have not spoken to another human being for weeks, except to order food, buy a ticket, or ask directions.

As I walk back into the town, I look at the walls on both sides of the narrow streets. People live hidden here, with huge carved doors in the walls, but only tiny openings cut into the closed doors. I am curious. I walk up to a small door left slightly open and peek in to see a garden courtyard,

"May I help you?"

I turn back to the street and see a boy with ivory skin, short hair and American style clothes. He is bowing respectfully, calling me madam, backing off slightly, then advancing shyly, as if eager to show his desire to help me without intruding. He must be a student. He looks no more than sixteen and stands nearly a head shorter than I. His English is excellent. He does not resemble my students either in language or appearance. My students are the poor and dark of this country. They come from the hungry villages or the dirty city streets. This boy comes from that other Mexico, the walled, protected part.

"You are lost?" he asks, keeping a distance of several feet between us, nodding his head anxiously.

"No. I was just walking. I was curious about that house."

He nods again, stands there. "I thought you were lost. You are from the U.S.?"

I nod, turn away and begin to walk.

He steps out in the same direction, close to the gutter, keeping five or six feet between us. "May I walk this way?" He spreads his arms. "I will go away if you want."

I see no reason why he should go away. It is ridiculous for him to act as if I might be afraid of him. I shrug. "Are you a student here?"

"Yes."

"In high school?" What is their equivalent of our high school?

He quivers, looks offended. "At university."

So, he is older than he looks, smooth and soft, protected, his adulthood held off, longer, a bit longer, not like my students who grow old so fast. Lately I too, have begun to look younger than other women in their forties, or so Arno said, telling me I grew younger during the war. It is only that I am thin. "What are you studying at the university?" I ask politely.

He looks uncertain. "Engineering." He says it with a shrug and a complete lack of conviction. "You would like a cup of tea, perhaps?"

Again, he backs off, spreading his arms as if to show he holds no weapons. "And let me practice my English on you," he adds, smiling happily at this inspired touch of respectability.

We find a table outside the hotel. He tells me he is twenty-three years old, has studied at the University of Mexico, and then here, for several years, off and on. Often he goes back to Mexico City. There, because he knows English so well, he can make a great deal of money as a tourist guide or transport agent. Of course, his family has money, 'but there are many children in the family to be educated, so there is no money to spare for good times. Mexico City is full of good times, "Too many good times, so my father sent me here, to sleepy Oaxaca. He says here I will concentrate more on my studies."

"And do you concentrate more here?"

"Sometimes."

He walks with me to the doorway of the hotel. "I am Manuel Luis Montez y Luzo. Manuel Montez." He puts out his hand and I shake it. It is a tiny, delicate hand. Everything about him is delicate and smooth. Like a doll.

"Anna Giardino," I say with a nod. "Thank you for the tea. I hope you will be successful in your studies." Then I turn and walk into the hotel.

That night I sit by the window with a book, occasionally looking up to watch the flickering lights and the promenading people. I follow one group of young people, counting five trips around the tiny Zocalo in one hour. That is a true feat of timing, to keep constantly in motion, yet cover so little ground. As I am smiling at this, I see one figure detach itself from the group and stand looking at my window. An arm is raised, then waved at me. It is Manuel. Before I can return the wave, he runs toward the hotel and disappears.

In a moment there is a knock at my door, and a note is handed to me: "I invite you please to come out and take a walk in the delightful night air." I laugh, put on a sweater and go out into the courtyard around which the hotel is built. He stands there grinning at me.

We do not promenade around the Zocalo. We walk straight across it and sit on a bench near where the band plays a sentimental waltz. It is so dark I cannot see his face. I wait for him to say something, but he is silent. Then, astonishingly, he takes my hand.

I pull back my hand, felling impatient and ridiculous.

"Oh, I am sorry, very sorry," he mutters.

And now I feel sorry for him. Oh, this is all too silly. "Manuel,

*really, I am old enough to be your mother, and besides. . . " I am at a
loss: it is simply too ridiculous.*

"I am only a child to you, " he says, his lips pouting.

"When you act this way, yes. "

"You looked so lonely, sitting there in the window. I thought. . . "

*That is unfair. I could slap him. "Yes, all right, I am lonely!" I
admit before I can think. "But that does not mean I. . . this is too
stupid. . . don't you see. . . " I stand up, but I don't move. I feel
uncertain, drawn, slipping into something. Someone has handed me a
script, the props are all arranged. "This is not what I want, " I say, but
I do not walk away from him. If I do, there will be no one to talk to.
"Stop making a fool of me. "*

*The lights flicker, the sticky-sweet music nudges my feelings.
Everything is saying, let go, don't think, just let things happen. No, it
is the wrong language, the wrong words, for the wrong woman.
If I let go now, if I sink into this, I will lose something important. . . something. I do not know what it is. But in some way,
I will be reduced if I take this. . . this vacation from my life, my self,
this amnesia, this dream, this trading of my total, whole identity for
this simple, sweet pretense. It would be a lovely rest, a lovely moment
of oblivion. But it would cheapen everything, my life, my pain, even
my loneliness, which it would erase, or blur. There is a conspiracy here
to take my loneliness (like my money) and offer in return some
cheap, assembly line, stamped-out imitation of what I need, like the
cheap trinkets in the Indian markets.*

*I want to tell him, to make him understand, but I can see, as he
turns his smooth face up to look at me, that he would not understand.
His face, in fact, is hurt, angry and shamed. "I am being made the
fool, " he says, "by you. To you I am only a stupid child. It does not
matter if you hurt me. While I, I would not hurt you, not for anything.
Tell me what you want of me, and I will do it. "*

*"I want. . . well, if you really want to be my friend, you could show
me the sights of Oaxaca, as a friend. After school, after you finish
studying. I want to see Monte Alban and. . . "*

*"Oh yes, I can do that!" He is instantly cheerful again. "In the
afternoon I have no classes. I will call for you at two. I will be your
friend. "*

*Each day he comes at exactly two and takes me to see a different
sight. He insists on paying for everything. He is formal, gentle, timid.
As he walks beside me in the street, people glance, then turn away.*

99

"That was my aunt. That lady with the black shawl. She sees me with you and does not speak to me." He looks pleased, a Don Juan with an illicit woman.

"I hope you are not neglecting your studies for my sake," I say, in clipped, schoolteacher tones. I wonder what that woman thinks of me.

He bows his head, but I can see the look of irritation on his face. Always there is this underlying irritation, this watchfulness. He has made a temporary concession, but he is waiting for me to give in. I ask him questions about his life as a student. He answers politely, then falls silent, not quite sullen, but sad, and waiting. We are caught in a still, silent struggle. I must hold the upper hand. But why? Why do I not just walk away from this struggle?

"Where did you learn to speak English so well?"

"At the movies!" Now he smiles. "When I am in Mexico City I see every American movie. All my life, I have seen every movie that comes. For a long time I saw only westerns. I used to say, 'I reckon,' and 'in these parts.' I thought that was real United States English."

As he tells me about the movies, I begin to understand his manner. He has absorbed not only the language of the movies, but a view of life shown in them. Life is a romance: boy meets girl. He is the boy. Faintly familiar phrases and gestures I now recognize, locate, in old movies. He is Errol Flynn, Gary Cooper, Clark Gable. But I am not Bette Davis!

The next time he tries to hold my hand, I make myself laugh and say, "Save that for when you go out with a nice Mexican girl your own age."

"A nice Mexican girl of my own age would not be allowed to go out with me." He frowns at me, narrows his eyes. "There are other kinds of girls, but I do not want to hold their hands." He is both subtle and obvious, manipulative, telling me my rejection may drive him into a brothel? Did he learn that one in the movies too?

There is something vulnerable and sad about him, and at the same time, something sinister. I am alternately attracted and repelled by him. I should tell him to go away. But I cannot tell him that lie anymore, that lie that I want him to go away. I have lost some ground already. He looks at me more boldly before quickly turning away when I look sharply at him. Each day I tell myself that this will be the last one. I will leave. But I stay on for one more day, one more day of gentleness, of quick, longing glances, of long silences.

He takes me walking through an old, empty churchyard. We sit on the wall looking over the dark town. He takes my hand, and I do not yank it back. He kisses me. so tentatively, so gently. I feel myself sliding into the role prepared for me, while part of me stands back, watching, commenting.

He pulls a ring off his finger and insists that I take it. "It is my high school ring." A blood red stone in etched gold. His hands are so slim and delicate that his fingers are no thicker than mine. The ring fits. Part of my mind says, "He must order these rings by the dozen and give them to American ladies he romances." No, I know that is not true, but it may be that in the future he will do so.

For I know now that he habitually neglects his studies, hoping for an adventure like this one, that he must cause great expense and heart-ache to his family. And I, I am taking him like a pill, a narcotic, to kill my pain. I make weak protests, knowing that my words are lies, or I would simply leave. "'You must not waste your time with me." (Hypocrite!) "You must study: in this country, there is nothing between the professions and poverty."

"There are the tourists." He is more blunt now. "More and more of them. Already I can make more money working for the tourist agencies than I would as an engineer, at least for a long time."

"Do you like tourists?"

He shakes his head. "Especially the ones from your country. They attack The Church, ask stupid questions, get sick on the food. They...oh, but not you, you are different. I have never known anyone like you." He looks at me with a mixture of cunning, innocence and need. He sighs like Charles Boyer, or is it Gilbert Roland?

And in the end he wins. Or loses? We both neither win nor lose. We simply act our roles. I bring it to an end, break this enchantment in the only way I can, by letting it destroy itself.

He comes to my room, late, in the dark, and makes love to me like what he is: a clumsy, rather spoiled boy. In five minutes it is over, the spell broken so suddenly that I shiver with the shock. The movie romance is over, ending as it never does in the old movies. I am no longer the treasured virgin, and he is suddenly a young male of a culture which values only the women it imprisons. I say something to him, and he answers me with a lazy, cynical voice totally unlike that of the boy who walked me up and down the sacred steps of Monte Alban. It is a tone so different and yet so familiar to me. It is...I gasp as I realize where I have heard it before. I sit up in bed, speaking into the darkness.

"When you spoke just now, do you know what I thought, what I saw in my mind? Those men, in the bars, in Mexico City. All the same, all pale and soft and fat, lighting the cigarettes of unhappy American women. I suppose that at home they have unhappy Mexican wives. They speak fluent English, like you. They make money. Perhaps the American women give them money. They give the women romance, attention, just like the movies, just like you... like what I let you be. They do it well, smoothly, professionally. And they look more bored, more lonely, more unhappy than the women."

Suddenly I am angry. "My God, if you were my son, I'd rather you became one of the starving peons, digging in the ground, than become one of those men. But it is so easy. So much easier than studying, so easy to be nice to the ladies who keep coming from the North, the unhappy ladies. Like me! It's my fault. I am older. I know. But even I couldn't resist. But you can. You're still young and haven't lost energy. It isn't your fault. But you must not be taken in, you must resist! Do you understand?"

I wait for an answer. For some sign that he understands what I am saying. In the darkness I hear only his breathing, heavy and even. He has fallen asleep.

I lie awake until the darkness begins to fade. Then I get up quietly and pack my clothes. I check out of the hotel as it is getting light, and stand for an hour in the cool morning sun waiting for the bus.

As the bus pulls out, I see him running across the Zocalo. *He calls my name. His eyes are wide, and he is sobbing, running after the bus as it picks up speed. Looking back at him I see, behind the contorted anguish in his face, a kind of dramatic exultation, like that of an actor who exults in the good performance of a very juicy role.*

Anna stopped her agitated swinging and held the chair still. She had never learned to rock in a rocking chair. Either she sat still or swung nervously to and fro. She was angry at herself. Here she was, trying to remember an important event of a few days ago, and instead she had drifted back to an irrelevant episode from twenty-five years ago.

Yet, in remembering it, she understood something for the first time, saw the Mexico episode as a door that closed off a part of her life. It was connected with the final closing off of the possibility of marriage. Probably she'd never really wanted marriage, family life. That explained her attachment to Arno, who, anyone could see, would never marry her. But she had never thought about the alternative. Then, entering the second half of her life, she saw the spectre of a loneliness deeper, a need more agonizing than she had ever expected.

What had happened in Mexico was like a preview of what her life might become. She could become a ludicrous figure, longing for tenderness and going, once or twice a year, to buy it in some place distant and poor enough to accommodate her. She had too much self-respect for that. Or, perhaps, she thought as she rocked more gently, it was only pride. Yet pride was something to keep when not much else was left. Married people, loveless as most of them lived together, were left with their pride. A single woman had to fight to keep hers.

It was a long hard fight. She knew that as her natural slenderness became more angular, as she turned off the responses in her body and mind, one by one, as she held herself, cool and alert, she was not really saving herself from humiliation. To show her need would be to open herself to humiliation as a silly old sexual beggar. To fight it and deny it only brought new humiliation: she was laughed at as a cold, frigid old maid.

Again, the roles were decided, prepared ahead of time. No matter what she did, she was pressed into one or the other. Was there no other alternative? If another existed, she thought, I never found it.

She was glad to have her thoughts interrupted by a knock on the door, a knock that was short and sharp, but followed by an insistent, almost desperate pounding. Only one person announced herself that way: Lydia. Anna got up, smiling and rather pleased with herself. Yesterday she could not even remember her neighbor, what had Arno called her? the witch. Today she recognized her even by her knock. Her mind was coming back. When she finally could remember what had happened to her on Sunday night, she would be quite all right.

"You are all right," Lydia declared as Anna opened the door. "I bring up the mail and some tea," she said, handing Anna some envelopes. She carried a pot of tea and two cups. Anna could smell the dry-grass, flat smell of herb tea. Lydia always insisted on making herb tea, mixing in thick globs of honey. Since Anna did not like sweet drinks any more than she liked herb tea, Lydia usually ended up drinking all the tea. "I could not come to see you in the hospital, of course," said Lydia, "But I see you come back all right." Lydia suffered from numerous allergies and other mysterious complaints which incapacitated her whenever she faced something she did not want to do. She would not even wear her glasses. She was always covered with bruises from bumping into things. She took huge doses of vitamin E and drank herb tea all day. But she filled her cup of tea with honey and ate chunks of milk chocolate and cheese, which both her doctor and her health magazines frowned on.

Anna had forgotten how harsh Lydia's voice was. She bore down on every word with her heavy German accent, as if she were pushing each one onto her listener, and her voice grated like the squeak of heavy machinery left unoiled.

They went into the dining room, sat across from each other at the old round table, and Lydia poured the tea. "I read about you in the paper. It reminds me of when poor Richard is hurt. He never regains consciousness." Richard was the husband she had been married to briefly fifty years ago. He was killed in a bar room fight after he had already left her. But Lydia never failed to declare her superior status of widow. It was a ritual that opened each conversation with her.

Lydia had come pounding on the door the day after Anna moved in, telling her all the things that were wrong with the house and with the neighbors. Anna managed to see little of her while she was working, but since her retirement Lydia had been harder to avoid. And she could not snub her without feeling guilty: Lydia had looked in on Mama every day during that last year.

Lydia aggressively made acquaintances, then complained about them, criticized them and eventually quarreled with them. Anna had never heard her say anything good about anyone and suspected she said cruel things about Anna to others. She had no telephone because she received threatening calls, she said, from people she had befriended, who turned on her. She read a great deal. She clipped accounts of burglaries or street violence and brought them to Anna. Some she mailed with the letters she wrote constantly to acquaintances or former friends she complained about. The only thing she loved was her cat, a fat, old, ill-tempered beast who scratched her, spat at her, would eat nothing but chicken livers and fresh crab, and was the cause of many of her allergic symptoms.

Lydia took a sip from her cup, then leaned back and began her usual recitation of rapes, accidents, murders, robberies, zestfully leading up to Anna's case. "Are you . . . molested?" she asked, leaning forward over the table.

Anna shook her head.

Lydia fell back in her chair. "How awful to be alone and old in a world like this. But you have at least me to count on. We are such friends this year, always our little tea. But I warn you so many times about walking, not safe, even in daytime. Nowhere is safe."

Such friends? Anna could not imagine that they could be called friends. Yet it was true that during the past year she sat with Lydia and her pot of tea nearly every afternoon. Anna wondered how she could have sat every afternoon listening to this woman pour out her quarrel with the world. She could not now stand five minutes of her voice.

"Do you know anything about what happened to me Sunday night?" Anna had to repeat the question three times before Lydia stopped her tirade against the noisy children who played ball in the street.

"Sunday night?"

"Yes, the night I was hurt. I don't know what happened. Did you see me that day?"

"Yes, of course, we have our usual little tea."

"What did we talk about? Did I say anything about plans to go out in the evening?"

"Say anything? No. But you never say anything. Not since we have become friends have you spoken much. You are a very inarticulate woman, but Italians, of course, are all. . ."

"I didn't say I was going out?"

"No. But you are always going out. I see you going out at night. I warn you not to, but. . ."

"Yes," Anna murmured. "It was because I couldn't sleep."

Lydia nodded. "Oh, I know."

"You know what?"

"That something is wrong. It is your nerves, from deficiencies, from eating and breathing all the poisons. How do you think I am seventy-eight and still strong?" She got up. Anna knew what she would do, her usual trick. She bent forward and touched the floor with flat palms. Anna laughed. The only pleasure this woman had ever given her was this ridiculous act. Lydia straightened up, glaring resentfully at Anna's smiling face. "If you will take vitamin E, you will not be so moody, so quiet and strange."

"Do you know what time I went out Sunday night?"

Lydia shrugged. "About midnight, as usual. Now you have learned your lesson, a lucky escape, you will listen to your friend. Have some tea. Open your mail." Lydia was curious about other people's mail.

There were two get-well cards from students Anna vaguely remembered. She passed the cards to Lydia, who brought them close to her face and studied them as if looking for clues to a riddle.

While Lydia examined the cards, Anna read a long letter from a stranger, an eighty-year-old lady who said she had been burglarized six times, and was afraid to leave her house. After this statement the letter wandered through four pages of memories, then broke off suddenly and was signed with only a first name, Susan. Anna looked at the name for a while. It was hard to visualize an eighty-year-old lady named Susan. Susan seemed to be a young name, while names like Eleanor or Anna were old names.

Lydia was watching her, waiting to see the letter, but Anna did not show it to her. To do so would be like putting the frail lady in Lydia's rough hands.

Anna picked up the last envelope. It was smudged and dirty, as if a child had handled it, a long envelope, but very thin. She could see that it contained a small piece of paper, hardly more than a scrap. There was no return address. Her name and address were printed in weak, lopsided letters, as if a right-handed writer had used his left hand.

She tore open the envelope and pulled out the piece of paper. She read the nine words scrawled on it and caught her breath. Then her heart began to pound, and everything blurred for a second. She folded the piece of paper.

Lydia had begun talking again and did not notice. "Like me, you are alone in the world, and they are poisoning the air, making the streets a..."

"I'm very tired," Anna said.

"...filthy battleground. Only yesterday I heard..."

"I'm tired, and I wish you would go now."

Lydia picked up her teapot and stood. She tried to express her outrage by standing stiffly and glaring down at Anna. But Anna was not looking at her. Lydia went to the living room, heading toward the front door, calling back in a harsh whine, "You want me to look in on you tomorrow?"

Anna did not answer.

Lydia slammed the door as she left, and Anna felt she had been added to the list of Lydia's former friends.

She unfolded the piece of paper. DIDNT GET YOU THIS TIME BETTER LUCK NEXT TIME She sat still for a few moments, breathing deeply, with her eyes closed, waiting for her heart to slow down. When she felt able, she got up, went to her bedroom and called the police. The officer she had spoken to in the hospital was not on duty, but they would send someone else.

An hour later she was talking to a stout, gray-haired man who lis-

106

tened to her and examined the note as if practicing a ritual he had gone through a thousand times. He questioned her about friends, relatives, acquaintances, neighbors, ex-students, anyone who might have a grudge against her. He referred to the letter-writer as "our crank," as if he offered to share any danger she might be in. Anna answered his questions carefully, always qualifying her answers by admitting she might not have a very clear recollection of anything, let alone Sunday night. By the time they were through talking, Anna was exhausted.

The man sat silently in a straight chair opposite Anna's rocker, looking at his notes, then shifting his gaze out the window. The sun was going down. A golden glow from the unseen sun yellowed the side of his face, then dimmed as patches of fog drifted in. "There are two possibilities," he said finally. "It could be that our crank is someone you know, perhaps very slightly, someone who imagines a grudge against you."

"A former student?"

The man shrugged. "The second possibility is that it's one of those random cranks, who probably doesn't know you, someone who read about you in the newspaper and decided to...have some fun."

"Fun! What kind of..."

"Miss Giardino, there are a lot of weird people in this world. You can't imagine. After twenty years on the force, I'm beginning to think everyone's a little crazy." He stood up, his back to the window. His face was in shadow and the light behind him was now all gray and foggy. "Chances are it's the second kind of crank. That's what it usually is, just some crazy person who sends letters or makes phone calls at random. He'll pick on someone else tomorrow. You'll never hear from him again. If you knew how many notes like this I've seen...and nothing ever comes of them."

"But if..."

"Of course, I'm turning in a report. I don't know how much protection we can offer you, unless we have something to go on. Unless you remember what happened Sunday night. Unless we can make a connection between that and this note. Or unless you know of someone who has it in for you. Meantime," he looked sternly at her, "stay off the streets after dark. Call us if you get another letter...or phone call." He spread his arms as if to say he could only tell her the obvious. "If you hear anything or remember anything more, call and ask for me. Okay?"

He took the letter with him when he left. She was glad. She did not want to have it in the house, the poisonous thing. Even if it came from a stranger, a crank who simply saw her name in the paper, it was terrible. Free, unattached hate, reeling about like a drunk man, hitting anyone who happened to be there. She could not let herself think about it. If she did, she would become like Lydia.

She went to the kitchen and cooked some eggs and toast. She could hardly keep her eyes open as she ate. Unlike Arno, she did not suffer many aches and pains; she felt her age in sudden waves of exhaustion that came over her without warning. As soon as she was through eating, she put her dishes into the sink and went to bed.

She closed her eyes, waiting for the sleep that would bring her more dreams. Dreams would give her the answers. She had picked up hints, shadows of memories from them before, like her recognition of Maria. And it seemed now more important than ever that she recover all her memory. All of it, even the part she felt afraid to remember.

It was only toward morning that she found her way back to her dream. This time she took careful note of all its parts: the building, the recognizable people on the roof, the flames shooting out of the dark windows. She seemed to be floating in the air at about the second story, then gradually rising. She floated upward to the fourth floor. She could see into the window of her old classroom. It was full of students. She knew they were recent students, students of her last few years of teaching, because they were mostly black and brown. They had pushed back the chairs and were dancing to deafening music. The music was harsh, hostile, mindless, furious, but their dancing was languid and sensuous, and they grinned stupidly. The only ones who did not dance and grin were those who stood against the walls, at first watching the dancers, but then turning away from them to scrawl obscenities on the walls.

Anna lost control. She forgot that she was watching her dream so that she could understand. She forgot that it was a dream. She hated their dancing and their mindless music and their obscenities. But she did not want them to burn. She screamed at them, but they did not hear. She waved her arms as if she were swimming breaststroke, pushing herself closer to the window. She yelled, "Fire! Stop playing and let me get you out of here. You'll all die in this place!"

The dancing went on. The music roared louder, blending with the roar of the fire.

But one deep, black voice, murmuring from somewhere in the dancing crowd, said quite clearly, "You get'n closer."

108

FRIDAY

ANNA AWOKE WHILE it was still dark, her jaw set, her stomach churning. The dream was fading, but her anger and exasperation faded more slowly. She tried to relax her aching jaw, reminding herself that it was ridiculous to remain angry at a dream. The anger faded, but only to make room for fear: DIDNT GET YOU THIS TIME BETTER LUCK NEXT TIME

She turned on the small bed lamp and looked at the clock near the bed. It was four-thirty. She decided she would read. She got up and wandered through the hall to the front room. She would look for something by her old friend, the clear, lucid and humane voice that provided a model for writing, for thinking, for living. She took one of her collections of Bertrand Russell's essays off the shelf and carried it back to bed with her.

She read the first few paragraphs of several essays before she gave up. She put the book down on the bed, leaving it open. So many years ago, the reasonable, kindly voice of Russell had been able to convince her that life could be lived, that learning made living possible. Even his final anti-war essays, in those last years before he died, when other protestors were shrill and half-crazed with frustration, were clear and rational, still a reassurance that life could be understood and dealt with even if Anna had not, as yet, done very well in her attempts to do so.

But, she thought, as she looked at the book lying open on the white sheet, his writing no longer reassured her. What was the connection she had once felt with him? She could not feel it now. He still seemed kindly and rational, but rationality, suddenly, seemed beside the point. He wrote like a man who had always been listened to, who expected his audience to be attentive, thinking and rational. Maybe people always had listened to him, admired him and respected him.

109

One might be a very different person, Anna thought, if everyone always listened.

She closed the book, turned off the light and tried to go back to sleep, but it was too late now. She got out of bed, dressed herself and put on her coat. There was a slight graying of the black sky, just a beginning of light. A good walk in the open air was what she needed. Surely it would be safe to go out now. There was even something a little defiant in her decision. No matter how frightened she became, she could not imagine letting her fears, even well-founded fears, deprive her of an activity that had always brought her pleasure and peace of mind.

She closed her door very softly and started down the stairs.

"Where in hell are you going?"

She looked down over the bannister to see Arno standing in his doorway. He wore a blue striped robe over pajamas. He began to cough, then turned abruptly and went back into his apartment, leaving the door open behind him. He obviously expected Anna to follow.

When she went in and closed the door, he was already coming back from the kitchen with a cup of tea in his hand. "I'm always awake before five now," he muttered, as he sat down stiffly. "Takes a few hours to get my joints creaking. You weren't going out?"

Anna shook her head. "I heard you up and thought I'd come down." It was easier to say this than to try to explain. He would scold her. He could still make her feel like a child, a poor Mission girl, ignorant of all the things "everyone" knew.

Arno nodded. "Good. Hell of a lot better than leaving me to rot down here alone."

There were no lights on in the apartment. They sat side by side on the sofa in the darkness.

"Have you any friends?" Anna suddenly asked Arno. It seemed natural to ask such a question in the pre-dawn dark. "I mean, anyone but me?"

After a moment Arno said, "No."

"All dead?"

Arno nodded, then said, "Never really had any. Acquaintances, lovers, wife, no friends. When we're young we think we have friends, but they're just people we bump into, rub against. Friends are rare."

Anna thought of Maggie, her friend during her first years of teaching. Maggie had married, and that was the end of their "bump-

110

ing into" one another. Who else was there? Men couldn't be friends with a woman, not a single woman. Except David. And single women, other teachers? Maybe Victorina was right: Anna had been too stiff, unapproachable, frightening other teachers as much as she frightened some students. Yet Maria seemed unafraid of her, had asked to see her again. Did that mean. . .

"I guess I haven't been a very good friend to you," Arno said. Anna did not answer. "That's not true," he said, as if she had agreed and he must defend himself. "The past few years, anyway, that last year before you retired, who else would have sat and listened to you spewing out that stuff day after day. I listened, let you get it off your chest every afternoon."

Anna nodded. "Yes, I remember those talks, when you put everything I said in political perspective, in the context of the collapse of Western Civilization."

"Well, that's where it all belonged."

"Maybe, but that wasn't much comfort to me when I had to go back the next day, up to that front door, past those groups huddled together, like football huddles ready to break and charge. They bunched in front of the door, pretending not to hear when I asked them to move. If you had run that gauntlet every time you entered or left the building, as I did, you might not have been so philosophical."

"You could have gone in one of the side doors the way the other teachers did."

"Never!"

Arno laughed. "That's my Anna. But then you stopped coming down to talk to me. From then on I might as well have been dead down here. Was it because of that argument? You were never one to hold a grudge. Did you hold that against me?"

Anna frowned. She did not remember any argument, so she could not say whether or not she held anything at all against him. That was the trouble with a shaky memory. The absence of something did not mean it was unimportant. It might mean just the opposite. "Which argument?"

"Oh, you were going into your usual thing on standards and grades and education being the key to upward mobility."

Anna nodded.

"And I told you it was a comfortable fiction, a way to keep the poor in their place. The few who rose proved the point, held out hope, but the whole thing was dependent on just a few making it."

111

Anna remembered. "And you said the students who were demanding the grades and degrees without the work, even the ones who cheated, who were threatening to make the whole thing break down, were right. It was rotten. It had to be destroyed and something new built. Working within it only perpetuated...*He's right! Oh, God, can he be right? It hits me like a blow, as if he'd doubled up his fist and struck with all his strength at my center. If he is right, then I made a terrible mistake, turned the wrong way, made my whole life, my life's work, a detour. By trying to save a few. That seemed possible, to save a few. How could I have faced it every day without a concrete goal? Limited. Reachable. So I pushed them all, preached salvation through education, hoping a few would listen and slip through. And when a few did, I felt vindicated, triumphant...righteous.*

I did my best. I used to repeat that over and over, through all these years of frustration, through all the ones I lost, all the failures. I did my best. I said it like a charm against evil, against fear. I did my best, my best. And now, does it turn out that my best was my worst? Was I only part of a murderous system? But I did my best. What else could I do? I did my best, as I saw it. My best!

Anna nodded. "You had taken my whole life, everything I struggled to do, and told me it was worthless."

"You always did take things too seriously."

Anna felt the sofa quivering as he shrugged. She turned her face toward his. The room was lighter, but still she could see only the outlines of his face, not its expression.

"I don't know how else to take things. Didn't you mean what you said?"

"Yes, but..."

"What you really mean is that I should just choose to ignore, to forget facts about myself that aren't very pretty. I know people do that, but I've never been able to figure out how they could."

"Life might have been easier for you if you learned how."

"I never wanted an easy life."

"Oh, Anna, so earnest, so serious, so intense. You've never changed...the first time I saw you at Cal, leaning across that table, arguing as if your life depended on it..."

"I must have looked silly."

"You looked beautiful! I should have married you. I should have picked you up from that chair, carried you off and married you. Then both our lives would have been different."

Anna shook her head. "You couldn't. You've never been able to stay around more than a couple of years. Then I'd have been an ex-wife and never seen you again. This way, I'm your friend, a life-long friend you drop in on from time to time."

"I don't like the tone of your voice. You've never been cynical."

"I'm not being cynical. I just..."

"Look, anytime you want me to go, you can just tell me."

Anna put her hand out silently and touched his, smoothing it gently and lightly. She felt his swollen and deformed fingers under hers and thought, two old claws touching in darkness. That was reality, not these pointless reminiscenses. "Once I get all my memory back," she said, "I want never to think about or talk about the past again."

They sat quietly for a few more minutes. Anna felt drowsy, relaxed. Soothing Arno had calmed her, made her forget for the moment the scrawled threat on the slip of paper. She decided not to tell Arno about it. It was better to try to forget it unless she received another. "It's getting light," she said. "I'll go back upstairs now." Arno did not answer her. He did not even move as she left.

Her apartment was cold. She turned on the heat and kept her coat on as she made herself some tea and boiled an egg. She broke the egg into a cup and continued walking around the apartment as she ate it.

Everywhere she looked, she saw the same things, the books. Once they had been a great comfort to her, but now she could think only of how dusty they had become. And some were, of course, quite useless, the old textbooks and most of the anthologies. She should get rid of those, at least. Now that she had thrown away all the teaching materials she brought home from Camino, perhaps she could learn to part with some of the books. But it would be hard to choose which ones to cull out. She had a sudden, almost mischievous thought of calling a book dealer and ordering him to take them all, all away for whatever he was willing to pay. The thought was exhilarating and frightening, rather like the thrill a gambler must feel when he loses, a kind of death, a kind of freedom.

Finishing the egg, she put the dish in the sink and filled it with cold water. Then she went to the rocker in the front window, wrapped a blanket around her legs and sat watching the city turn bright.

Ringing. The phone. She opened her eyes. As she went to the bedroom she glanced at the clock. It was after eight o'clock. "Hello."

"Oh, I woke you."

"No, David, no, I've been up since quite early. But I guess I dozed off in the rocking chair."

"How are you feeling?"

"Very well."

"No unexpected aftereffects?"

"None."

"And the memory? You've recalled what happened?"

"Not that. Not yet. But otherwise my memory is mostly restored. After all, how much do people my age remember?"

"Or even care to?" said David. "Look, my dear, I hope you'll forgive me for not looking in on you again, but things have been moving rather fast. I have a buyer for the Clay Street house."

"Already?"

"Well, it seems they've had their eye on it for some time. A foundation. They're buying it to use as a half-way house for drug addicts and convicts. Paying quite a decent price."

"And once it's sold. . . ."

"There are just a few details about transferring funds, and then I'm off."

"You're really going for good." Anna had not really believed it. It would take a while for the reality of his going to reach her. Now, she thought, if I am Arno's friend, David is my friend. Even when he was away on one of his trips, he kept in touch, and she knew that if at any time she had written that she needed him, he would have come back. But David was getting old now too, and would settle permanently in France. He would never come back.

"Yes, well, the truth is, I must. I can't afford to live here on what I shall have. I shall just scrape by there."

"I'll miss you."

"Then come visit me! You're free to travel now: a good retirement income, no responsibilities."

"Perhaps."

"I'll be tied up until Sunday, but I want to see you then. May I come about noon?"

"Of course. We'll make it a farewell party."

"Oh, no, that sounds too sad. See you Sunday."

Almost as soon as she hung up, the phone rang again. When Anna heard the voice, she recognized it immediately although she had not heard it since she retired.

"Miss Giardino. Stewart Warner."

"Yes."

"I heard you had . . . an accident or something."

"Something."

"Like to come by and see you this afternoon." There was a false heartiness in his voice, contradicted by a kind of whine in the last word.

"That's very kind of you."

"Well, see you about three." A hesitation, then a click and the buzz of disconnection.

Anna was sure she knew exactly what had happened. Stewart Warner had been called to the principal's office. As head of the English department, he was delegated to visit her. He would make his visit, stay twenty minutes, then go, and she would not hear from him again. Everyone would be satisfied that the right thing had been done. No one but Anna would see the irony of it. *"Grammar is the mythology of English."*

"What's that supposed to mean?" I look at this young man, Stewart Warner. His name sounds stern and strong enough, the first man in the department since Mr. Ruggles retired. But he has a loose look about him.

"It means . . . well, some things are the sort of esoteric or abstract type of thing that . . . "

Sort of. Type of. He doesn't know what he means. He just picked up the phrase somewhere. I can help him. "I agree with you," I say. "I drill them in grammar, yes, but it's reading that will teach them how to write, to think. It's reading, reading and more reading."

"Oh, now . . . " He shrugs that loose shrug. "It's possible to live too much in books, you know. Books aren't life."

"Of course they're not. But the ability to read is the most important thing we can give our . . . "

"For facts, yes, if you're talking about facts."

"I'm talking about education. At least, I thought that was what we were talking about."

"Education is a means, Miss G. Not an end in itself."

"Granted. And the end . . . ?"

He shrugs again as if patiently reciting the obvious. "Why, happiness, adjustment to a reasonably fruitful set of relations with one's peers, one's family, one's . . . world." He swings his arms out as if to embrace the world, but they flap too limply to hold anything. He smiles

115

an empty, easy smile. He is so relaxed, he might just fold up like an accordian.

"But aren't there certain facts and skills, like reading, that they have to learn in order to be happy and adjusted, to be able to earn a living, for instance, or to vote intelligently, or. . ."

He shrugs, flaps his hands, mumbles phrases containing words like insight, understanding and, always, adjustment. I don't understand, and I wonder if he does.

I thought, when salaries went up and the war ended, bringing the men back into teaching, things would be better. Most of the women I work with are poorly educated, unimaginative, lazy. Are they, as Arno says, merely the unmarriageable daughters of politicians? Some are. Are they from "better" schools, exiled for incompetence? Some are. Did they start out dull and bored? Some did. Or did they try and try, and just get worn down? Some did. Now comes this man, and others like him. They all have minors in psychology, and they all talk about adjustment, understanding. Stewart Warner is always understanding everything, absorbing everything like a limp sponge. He seems to think that perfect psychological adjustment is lack of reaction, that anything resistant is neurotic, another favorite word of his. His limp, uncomprehending understanding drives me into a fury, and he knows it does.

I study Stewart Warner and learn about him. I learn that he never assigns homework. "Six hours of schooling a day is enough."

"Yes," I tell him. "Six hours ought to be enough if this place were devoted to disciplined study, but. . ."

I learn that Stewart Warner never gives a grade lower than a C. "Anything lower would be psychologically damaging."

"More damaging than not learning to read and write? Mr. Warner, our students come out of homes where little English is spoken, and off streets where people who carry a book are laughed at. The pressure of grades is sometimes the only pressure to counter that. Some students even welcome. . ."

I learn that Stewart Warner will, eventually, when he becomes department head, solve the problem of our disagreement by creating a gilded ghetto for me. "Miss Giardino, the principal has agreed to give you all the seniors who are college bound."

"Why? So that I can mop up the messes left by lazy teachers? So that, when all this life-adjustment nonsense catches up with them, they come to me to learn how to read and write?"

116

Anna found herself pacing back and forth, shaking her head, mumbling words from old arguments, repeating old things she had said and some she hadn't said. She tried to stop, but couldn't. The old frustration dogged her, nagged her, drove her, so that when Stewart Warner knocked at her door, she swung the door open ready almost to shout at him.

He took her by surprise. His hair was quite gray. A big man, he looked paunchy and tired, as if weary of carrying his own weight. What used to be a casual incline of his head, inviting relaxed confidences, had become a definite stoop. Stewart must be in his mid-fifties now. She had always thought of him as young and new, but surely he must have been aging while she saw him every day before she retired. Somehow he'd never shown it until now. The sudden aging of her enemy disconcerted her.

"You look very well," he said, shaking her hand. "And always the same. Ageless. I don't think you've changed at all in the. . .what is it . . .twenty-odd years we've known each other."

"You've aged," said Anna.

He shrugged, giving just a hint of the noncommital, loose expression which used to infuriate Anna. "Well, these last few years. . ." His voice trailed off in the same way it always had, leaving heavy possibilities which had to be guessed at. "But are you all right? We were very concerned to hear. . ."

They sat near the window, Anna giving him the rocker and taking a straight chair for herself. It seemed more natural for him to be gently rocking this way. "Yes. I wasn't injured."

"Exactly what happened? The newspaper. . ."

"I've been trying to find out. The shock blanked out my memory, but that's been coming back. The police are no help. Nothing was stolen." Anna paused. "It could have been someone who wasn't after money. . .someone who knew me."

"Oh, well, now. . ." No, he had not changed. He always shook his head that way when he heard something he did not want to hear, did not want to think about. She thought of telling him about her crank note just to see how he would manage to shake that out of his head.

"Attacks on teachers aren't unusual," she said. "What about that woman who came right into a classroom and nearly killed that teacher with an icepick. What about those gangs roaming the halls?"

"You think it was a student?"

"Weren't there some who hated me?"

"But not enough to..."

"Remember that boy...what was his name? The one who told you I was ruining his life because I didn't give him an A. His father called me at home and threatened me. And didn't the Black Students' Union ask that I be fired because I was racist? Racist because I made them conjugate verbs?"

"I didn't know you knew about that."

"And the ones on drugs. Every time I threw one of them out and said no one came into my room without all his faculties, I made everyone angry, including you. No one could understand why I wasn't grateful if some of them slept through my class. 'At least the stoned ones are quiet,' everyone said."

"So you could have been stoned by the stoned." He grinned, but Anna did not smile back. He always evaded awkward questions by making feeble jokes.

"Why did you come?" she asked.

"Because we were concerned...because we all..."

"Oh, stop it, Stewart." It was the first time she had ever called him by his first name. "You're here because Jimmie Smith told you to come. It's one of your duties as department chairman. Well, you've done it and can report back that I'm still alive, that I haven't changed, that I'm still the indestructible, reactionary, hatchet-faced old maid. Your words. You didn't think I'd ever overheard you, did you?"

For a long time Stewart Warner sat quietly rocking as if he had not even heard what she said. He rocked absentmindedly like a tired old man. Then he began to nod.

"You're right, Jimmie did suggest I come. But I'm not department chairman anymore. At least I won't be at the end of this year. I resigned from that job. I'll be in the counseling office." He grinned sheepishly. "Shuffling papers." He gave an apologetic chuckle. Classroom teachers, even enemies like Anna and Stewart, agreed that most counselors were overpaid file clerks who had less contact with students than the janitors had. "And there've been some changes in the retirement regulations, early retirement at a little less money. I can retire in a couple of years."

Anna was surprised. "You want to leave the teenage world? You used to say you were lucky to live and work in an adolescent atmosphere. That the students kept you young." Anna laughed. "I used to feel that they aged me by decades every day!"

He looked at her directly. This expression was new. It seemed to

118

Anna that he never had looked directly into her eyes before. "The students don't relate to me anymore." Relate. Couldn't he just say they didn't like him? "In the beginning I was like a big brother. Then, after forty, you're a kind of father image. But the last few years... when you get past a certain age, they don't...but you know what I mean."

Anna shook her head. "I was never their sister or their mother. I was their teacher. I used to make sure they quite understood that."

"But some of them liked you."

"As teacher...not sister or mother or friend, or girlfriend or... anything else. As teacher. An entirely different sort of relation, and in certain ways much more intense and personal." She waited for a reaction, but it was clear that Stewart did not understand what she was talking about. She shrugged. "But most of them hated me."

"Well, I wouldn't go so far as..."

"Hated me and then loved me...as a teacher. Because I was hard and strict. It took about six weeks. For six weeks they feared and hated me because I was attacking them. I was going to make them change, and change is frightening. It was an attack on what they were. Then, one day, they'd all come together, all in my hands, on my terms, all loving me for having made them learn, for showing them they could learn, for making them beautiful. People are beautiful when they are learning." Anna sighed. "But then, as the years went by, it took longer than six weeks, and longer, and longer. And fewer became beautiful. They stayed sullen, resistant..."

"Perhaps because, like me, you were getting older, and the students couldn't relate..."

Anna shook her head. "I blamed you."

"Me?"

"For undermining me. Whether you openly said it or not, you conveyed to the students your opinion that my strictness was cruel, that my demands were unkind, that my...my style was inhumane. Oh, don't disagree. We've battled so many times. You won, the father-confessor style won, and the strict style lost."

"Won...lost...I don't know." He rocked silently for a few minutes. "It might make you feel better if I tell you something. Our newest teacher...very popular. His...his style is...I guess it would be called political. Psychology is a middle-class plot. Adjustment is conformity. Tolerance is acquiescence. Anyone who isn't attacking... attacking something, it doesn't seem to matter what...is a tool of The

119

System."

Anna understood. A new style was in, and Stewart's style, as well as hers, was out. He was going through what she did in her last years. He'll go more quietly, she thought, not raging and fighting as I did. But it's the same. Did he think that it would give her satisfaction to hear that? How cruelly he judged her, despite his kindly look. How little he knew her.

Stewart went on rocking, his head inclined to the left, his vague gaze directed out the window across the rooftops. "I'm getting old, I guess," he said. Anna turned her head away. Something in the way he shook his head and repeated the phrase made her feel ashamed for him. She had heard it said this way, with the same gestures, by so many people, throughout her life, the same helpless, "I get old, I get old," that her mother had murmured with an apologetic smile. And he not even sixty yet!

"But things are not bad this year," said Stewart, looking more cheerful. "Haven't had a riot, not one." He stopped rocking and leaned forward. "I thought you might be interested in some of the changes since Jimmie Smith took over. Let's see, he came during your last year, so he's been principal nearly five years now. Did you have Jimmie as a student?"

Anna nodded. "Quiet, melancholy boy. Read a lot. Barely passed composition. Read history. Not the type to become an administrator. That's a compliment, of course."

"I don't even remember him," said Stewart, "though he says he was in one of my classes. Well, he taught at Poly for ten years, then at Balboa. I don't think he ever would have made principal except no one else wanted it, not the way things were that year. Oh, and his mother, it turns out, was Mexican, so that put him ahead of all the athletic coaches for an administrative job."

"And you say he's solved the problems," Anna said. "How did he perform this miracle?"

"A lot of changes," said Stewart. "For instance, new program. I brought you a copy." As he drew the paper out of his pocket, his face became lively, as though he had not, just a few minutes before, confessed that he wanted to get out of the classroom as soon as he could. Even Anna felt a surge of interest as she reached for the paper. The Teacher's Reflex, she thought, hope seen in any variation of curriculum or scheduling. "You see, with flexible scheduling and all these new offerings..." Anna saw that the titles English I, English II, and so

120

on had been replaced by titles like "Science Fantasy" and "Diary Writing," and that the time blocs were shorter and irregularly spaced. "Quite a change, eh?"

Anna slowly nodded her head, feeling suddenly tired, as if about to be attacked by one of her waves of total fatigue. She had seen it all before, when she was in high school, in the days when classes were named by subject content and scheduling was irregular. When she began teaching, The Depression forced staff cuts, so classes were merged and homogenized into first year English, second year English, and so on. The war finished the flexible schedule and locked everything into the identical daily time slots, like the parts coming off the assembly lines in the great munitions factories. Stewart hadn't started teaching till after the war. He didn't know.

"And here's another thing," Stewart went on gaily. "No more cut slips and hall duty and calling the truant officer. You should have seen Jimmie at the last PTA meeting saying, 'You can't expect us to baby-sit your kids and account for them every minute of the day.' Remember, Miss Giardino, how you used to say if you could throw one troublemaker out of class you'd have ten times more energy to teach the others?"

"So there's no attempt to enforce the compulsory school law anymore."

Steward nodded. "Nobody has to come if he doesn't want to. Result: less milling around the halls, fewer trouble makers in class, no more. . . why, it's eased all kinds of tensions, including the ones we thought were racial. Of course, we've had to get security guards because there's still the problem of outsiders coming in to make trouble, and theft is about the same, but fires are down." He stopped and smiled at Anna, waiting for her reaction.

She began to laugh. You can't expect us to baby-sit your kids. That was the kind of thing Mr. Ruggles would have said. Fifty years later, she thought, they have decided he was right. If we keep making these marvelous discoveries, these great progressive strides, she wondered, will we eventually end up with something like what schools were before I was born? Are we all going backward to move forward? Or do we just go in circles? And end up where we started, tired and dizzy.

She could not stop laughing.

Stewart smiled and nodded. He went on nodding until he realized that Anna's jaw was trembling, the way it had trembled the time she

121

screamed at him that the next time he said "motivation" as if it were a mysterious gift which she refused to bestow upon the students, she'd try bringing a few sticks of dynamite to motivate them.

"I'm sorry, I can't help it." She had stopped laughing. Her voice was very low. "Then it was all a mistake. All the roll sheets I checked, all the intimidation from the principal, all the sullen hatred from the ones who wanted out, all the times I was told a really good teacher didn't have behavior problems, all the desperate parents, all the times I threw a student out, only to have him come back with a pat on the head from the principal. The way I learned to stand, to look, to hold them with my eyes, all the energy, all the precious energy."

Stewart did not move. He had stopped rocking, and his head sat straight on his stiff neck. Anna swallowed. "I'm sorry, Stewart. I didn't mean to...I'm not angry at you."

Stewart smiled, perfectly relaxed again. Anna realized that her anger could never match his formidable tolerance, the dullness he armoured himself with. She was about to tell him that Camino was still far from a paradise for conscientious teachers, but she did not want to betray anything that Maria had told her.

As if reading her mind, he said, "Maria told me she came to see you. That brings me to the second reason I came. To ask you something."

"What?"

"You know, Camino's centennial is coming up next year. There are plans, of course, for a great reunion party, and at least five other ceremonies. Jimmie Smith wanted someone to write a history of the school. That's right, a book, about yearbook length, with some old photos. When Maria reminded me how long you've been around here, I thought, who could be better? You've spent your whole life, practically, in The Mission."

"That's true." It took a moment for Anna to realize the truth of it. "That's true," she repeated. "When I was a student, Mr. Ruggles told me to study and go to college or I'd never get out of The Mission. But I never did get out, even though I did what he told me. That must mean something. What does it mean?"

Stewart pulled himself up out of the rocking chair. "I can bring you what material we have. A lot was lost in the 1922 fire, and there's never been any systematic keeping of records, but..."

"No." Anna shook her head. "I don't think I'm the person to write it."

"But who else has your length of. . ."

"Oh, anyone could piece together a few dates and write what Jimmie wants. You said it, like a yearbook, a sentimental story to be read by alumni. I wouldn't write it that way. I'd write about what really happened."

Finally she had reached him. Almost for the first time Anna saw apprehension on Stewart's face. It made her laugh again. He stiffened, afraid of her laughter. He thinks I'm crazy, Anna thought, and laughed even harder before she was finally able to stop.

She put out her hand to shake his. "Tell Jimmie Smith I'm glad about the changes he's made. Tell him I wish him success. Tell him if I were starting all over again, I'd want to work with him."

She did not look at Stewart Warner again. She did not get up from her chair. She heard his goodbyes only faintly, as she heard the opening and closing of the door. She sat straight and still, looking out over the city as her words echoed in her mind: starting again, again. *I stand in the front of the room, leaning back against the wide desk, looking across the room, across the rows of empty student desks, heavy wooden desks with broad writing surfaces, holes for obsolete, vanished ink wells, deeply scored surfaces. All the other teachers have new student chairs, chrome and plastic. But I love these old, heavy wooden chairs, and I demand that I be allowed to keep them.*

Tomorrow the students will come, and I am ready. The assignment is already on the board. (They will groan at the sight of a homework assignment on the very first day). I have a new writing idea for the poetry unit, and my new exercise on subordination must be the answer, must work, this time. The trouble is that a new device always works, for some of them, the first time. Then, with use, it works less well, and I must find another way, and another. What does it mean? That doors open into their minds and then close again? Never mind. This time, this method will work.

I stand here like an actor in the wings, waiting to go on. No, not an actor, not ready to pretend, perform. But there is excitement. Perhaps like the excitement of an artist with a huge rock, ready to carve, an artist seeing already the form within the rock, the form waiting to be brought out. I always begin this way, facing wide possibilities. A few weeks from now, this feeling will begin to erode away. And at the end of the year I will be tired and disappointed that what I saw, the possibility of form that I saw. . . has not come, not this time.

How can I start this way, year after year, with this excitement, this hope, when I know, I know how it will all end in exhaustion, in dis-appointment, in failure. Yes, always in failure, really, so few results from the effort put forth, so little done, so little. . . and yet the excite-ment is here as I look at these empty chairs, and the hope. The hope always comes back.

She ached from sitting so long. She got up and stretched. Perhaps she would go out a bit now, walk at least around the block. She went downstairs, out the front door, through the garden and half-way down the stone steps.

Then she saw the three mailboxes hanging on the concrete wall. Through the holes in the front of her mailbox, she saw white. There was mail. She was almost afraid to look, but she hesitated only a moment before lifting the flap at the top of the box and pulling out the envelopes. There were several ads and a letter addressed to her in a handwriting she did not recognize. But, she reassured herself, it was not lopsided printing; it was a good, firm, honest handwriting. The envelope was postmarked Los Angeles.

Turning it over she read the name and address of the sender: Stephen Tatarin. Stephen. Was it Stephen? After all these years, had she, by thinking of him, performed some magic that brought a letter from him? She was almost more hesitant about opening this letter than she was when she stood before the mail box afraid of finding another threat.

She carried the letter back upstairs, threw away the ads, and then sat down in the rocking chair to read it.

> Dear Miss Giardino:
>   I have just spent an incredible three hours, in thirty-five year old memories, where I was thrown after reading about you in the news clipping my sister sent me. I picked up the phone a few times, but talking to you on the phone after so many years seemed impos-sible. I might not be able to say on the phone the things I want to tell you. I am sorry you were injured. But I'm glad the incident pushed me to write, to tell you things I might not have thought of until, perhaps, I heard of your death some time in the future. Or perhaps I might die before you, leaving much unsaid. It seems hard to realize that we, only 12 years apart, are contemporaries now, instead of a woman and a boy.
>   First of all, about myself. After I left school there was still the depression, and then the war. But after the war I was able to go to college on the GI bill. I majored in psychology hoping, mainly, to find help in making sense of my own life. For the past fifteen years I have done counseling and therapy, helping others, I hope, as well

as myself. My second marriage took, and the oldest of my three children is in college.

So life has gone well for me, better than you might have expected. That is good news for a teacher, isn't it? I'm not wrong, am I? in believing that teachers gain some validation for their lives and their work in hearing that a former student is okay. For a teacher can always claim some credit for the successes of her students.

In my case much of the credit goes to you. I am not speaking of the subject matter you taught me, though surely that was valuable. There was something beyond the respect for reading and writing I got from you, though I'm not sure I can find the right words to describe it.

It was what you were, rather than any specific thing you taught me, that became a standard for me. What a teacher is can't be hidden or faked; it is there, day by day, in that intimate and intense contact of daily class work. There were days when you were tired, days when you were frustrated, days when the students who were unready (and might always be) to accept what you offered, must have been unbearable. There was your personal life, of which we knew nothing, but which could not have been easier than that of most people.

But you were the same every day: strict, demanding, impartial and fair. You were as certain as the sun rising each day. And, I suppose, most students thought of you as a natural phenomenon rather than as a human being. No young person knows what it costs to be so egoless, to remain consistent, no matter what the pressures. We only learn this by growing older, if we ever learn it. Whether or not we ever do learn it depends a great deal, I think, on the memory of successful examples, which encourage us as we try and fail and try again.

In impossible conditions you fought to do your work. You fought for us (though at times you appeared to be fighting with us). Even then, as a boy, I could see this and admire it because I too (in my confused and scattered way) was fighting.

That was why we loved each other.

I want to be clear about that. I am not talking about a so-called schoolboy crush, a nasty term which, I am glad to say, I have never used to describe the emotions of the young. I am fifty-six years old now and have known passion, but never any stronger than what I felt for you at the time, and what I knew you returned. I dreamed of you. I dedicated everything I did to you. I woke each morning waiting to see you.

I can still see you, tall and slim, taking long strides down the hall, your face clean and tanned, your eyes sharp and intense behind your glasses. You had just cut off your long hair, not to adopt the stylish waves women glued to their heads in those days, but in a wild, boyish chop, as if to cut your head free from any restraint. I used to imagine running with you. Always in my fantasies we were in motion, in passionate, purposeful motion. Passion surrounded you like an aura. I could almost hear it crackling like electricity. I wondered if I, who loved you, was the only one who could see it. I believed I was. I believed that, in loving you, I had tapped into that passion, and fed and grew on it.

I still believe that. And so, what I wanted to tell you is this. There have been many times, bad times in my life, when the memory of sharing that passion was my only assurance that I had something in me, something worth living for. I knew (this sounds absurd as I write it, but still it is the truth) that there was something of worth in me, because I had loved you so strongly.

I consider myself very lucky to have had this...whatever it is ...awakened by you, merged with yours, held gently and responsibly by you. I am very lucky that, in a deeper sense than is usually meant by the words, we have been lovers.

I'm not going to read this over, because if I do I might decide not to send it. I might send instead a safe, polite wish for your recovery. I might begin to fear that all I have said was only in my imagination, and that you may look at my name without even being able to remember who I was.

But I tell my clients they must learn spontaneity, make a mistake rather than squash a response, learn to trust their intuition, and over my doorway I have printed Blake's, "If a fool would persist in his folly he would become wise."

And so I will be, like my beloved teacher, an example of what I preach.

Stephen Tatarin

She had to wipe her eyes to read the last few lines, and her vision immediately blurred again. When she finished reading, she went back to the beginning and read the letter again, this time her tears falling faster than she could wipe them away, the blurring making her stop frequently. Some parts she read aloud, and her voice, despite her crying, was full and strong as she passed the words through her throat, her mouth, out into the air around her.

When she finished the second reading she let the letter fall to her lap and let her tears fall freely. They were not sad or sentimental tears, and there was only a mild expression of gratitude in them. The tears gushed out in release of something Anna could not have named. It was as though a great stiffness in her body had melted and now poured from her.

After a while the tears stopped abruptly. She sat still. She wanted to remember this quiet, still, empty feeling, for it would surely pass after a while. She must remember it if she were to regain it once it was gone.

She was glad that, for the rest of the day, no one called her. She moved quietly about the apartment, ate a little, then went to bed early. She stretched and yawned. Her body relaxed almost voluptuously, almost as if it were young and pliant again. She fell quickly and deeply asleep.

Searching, she was searching Camino Real High School, looking for Stephen. She went from room to room. Each time she opened a door, she faced a person or a scene she recognized from her years there. Sometimes everything was all mixed up. Classes were made up of students she'd had twenty years apart. Students rose to report on books she had never heard of and handed her papers written in a strange language. In one classroom sat all of the principals she had worked under. She stood in front of them sternly but patiently trying to explain something, but they all grinned and shrugged sheepishly, unashamed and cheerful, poking each other and laughing. "Hopeless," she said, as she left that room.

Out in the halls the students gathered in little groups and gave her sideways, sometimes menacing glances. She held herself very straight and pretended not to notice them. They might at any moment attack her, especially if they knew she had any idea of their intention. She must ignore them, pretend that she did not care that they hated her. She must think of Stephen, only Stephen, remember only that she was searching for him.

But then she realized that he could not be here. "Of course, he's gone; I helped him get out." And she realized that Stephen was not the person she should be searching for. Thoughts of Stephen were a detour from her real search.

Everything darkened, as if someone had turned out the lights in the hall. She groped her way along the wall.

Room after room she searched, and each time she opened a door she felt more dread at what she might find. Her weariness and her fear grew together. She was tired of searching and afraid of what she would find if her search were successful.

And then she knew she was dreaming. I am only dreaming, she thought, dreaming the search for that last bit of lost memory, the memory of what happened to me on the street in front of the school. Why am I afraid? Am I afraid of the fear, the pain? But I won't really be reliving it. It is only a dream, a dream I know I am dreaming, safely.

127

She tried to move faster, to open more doors, glance in quickly at the jumbled scenes her memory assembled, then shut the doors and go on. She forgot she was dreaming, then reminded herself again, then forgot again. She kept moving.

Finally she found herself in front of the big front door. She grabbed the metal bar and pushed the door open. Outside was dark, utter blackness. She could see nothing. She forced herself forward, through the doorway, out onto the broad steps. She heard the door crash shut behind her.

She stood frozen with panic. There was someone behind her. Someone who had been following her throughout her search. She felt his breath on her. She recognized his voice, softly murmuring, "Here I am." And she could not make herself turn to face him.

SATURDAY

"I KNOW WHO it was."

Arno sat back on the mottled couch and gave a loud sniff. His attention was complete.

"His name is Booker Henderson. Booker T. Henderson." Anna had had countless Booker T.'s, the name expressing parents' hopes, the name repudiated by its bearers. "It was during my last year. First period senior English." Anna paced back and forth as she talked, as if keeping her body in motion would keep her mind moving toward a complete answer. "He was late every morning. Never turned in any work. I checked his record and found all C's and D's. Which would have been all F's thirty years ago. Forty years ago he wouldn't have been in school at all. I tried to talk to him, but he was always the first one out, after the few minutes he spent in class. When I gave him an F for the first report period, I got a call from his counselor, who said Booker had to come from Hunter's Point. So do others, I said. He'll have to leave home earlier, I said. Then came the delegation from the Black Students' Union, saying I had no respect for Black Dialect. I told them I wasn't sure what dialect Booker wrote, since he had never turned in any work, and, in any case, I was qualified to teach only standard English...to students who attended my class. Then another counselor, saying Booker suddenly wanted desperately to go to college, and they were so glad to see him caring about something, couldn't I give him another chance? I said the question was rather that he had not given me a chance. Vague promises, then, about getting him to class on time."

"Did he come?"

Anna nodded. "Every day, more or less on time, for about two weeks. He sat in the back of the room. And watched me." She sat down, suddenly limp, exhausted. "Watched me. Glared at me."

129

Hatred. Murder in those eyes. Death rays shot out at me. Death rays. Enormous energy, gathered together with frustration and fear. And aimed at me. Unreasoning, unquestioning, self-indulgent, stupid. But satisfying. Yes, he enjoys gathering up all this fury and aiming it at me, the one simple, easy, accessible target.

If I told him my father was a slave destroyed by The System, would he listen? If I told him we are both victims? If I told him he is enjoying this in order to avoid the harder work of doing something about it? If I told him...no, I've tried, tried, so many times, with so many. He won't listen. They never listen.

"No one," Anna said, "pointed out to Booker that he might use that energy learning something from me. They just shrugged and said that was how black students felt, instead of telling him those feelings were just another excuse for not facing his illiteracy and doing something about it!"

"I guess the solution is black teachers for black students," said Arno.

"He'd had black teachers, and didn't do any better work for them. Besides, some of the black teachers they were hiring, just because they were black, weren't much more literate than Booker." Anna sighed. It was the old story, not only of waves of poor illiterate students, but of waves of teachers hired in response to transient political pressures. No point in going into all that again.

"So what happened?" said Arno.

"He finally turned in one paper. Full of hate. Full of errors, misspellings, wrong verbs, commas scattered irrelevantly, like bird droppings. But when I saw it, I knew. I knew I could do it."

"Do what?"

"Teach him." How could she explain? The thought behind the paper was pure hate, but it was clear. All the errors were mechanical problems. There were no sentences that fall apart in the middle because the mind can't sustain a thought. There was no hopeless collapse or sudden emptiness or hysterical explosion. No one could understand without having read paper after paper and learned to recognize the mind so damaged that a teacher could do very little. Whatever damage Booker had suffered, and she was willing to admit he had suffered much, it was reversible. He was still strong. She could do something for him. She could begin. "He was," she said simply, "teachable. Possibly very intelligent. You can tell, when you've read a lot of papers."

"So what happened?"

"The usual." She got up and looked out the window. "They wouldn't let me."

"Who wouldn't let you?"

She turned to Arno. Her voice dropped. It was low and tired, weighted. "I spent an hour on that paper, gave it back to him, told him to rewrite it with all the errors corrected. He was furious. He wanted me to react to what he'd said, wanted me to hate him in return for the hatred he'd written at me, wanted me to give him an F, give him one more excuse to hate instead of to learn, to work.

"He was on that edge, that edge whole classes used to be on, hating me because I threatened to change them, demanded work of them, demanded growth. That edge, where they would have to let go. Oh, they could pretend to hate me, outside of class, make fun of me, call me the old maid battleaxe, but in class they'd have to let go, secretly, one by one, they would give in, surrender, and let me teach them.

"But his hatred was so strong. And I...well, I was sixty-four years old. I needed help. When he took his paper from me, called me a racist bitch, walked out slamming the door with enough force to break its window, if the window weren't already broken and boarded up...I needed help. From his counselor. From the principal. From the Black Students' Union. Support from anyone who would..."

"From anyone," Arno supplied, "who would take him aside and say, 'Booker, you're full of shit.' "

"But no one did. No one had the courage to stand up against the shoddy slogans."

"What happened?"

"He dropped out of school. Blaming me. They let him go! Rather than support me. I was too perfect a scapegoat. Talk about injustice! When I started teaching I was looked down on and called a dago. When I ended my teaching I was looked down on and called a racist."

Arno waited while she sat down again. "Well, now, that brings us up to Sunday night. Did he follow you? Or was it a chance meeting? Did he have a weapon?"

Anna shrugged. "I don't know."

"Well, describe what happened."

"I still don't know what happened. I know it was he, because of my dream."

"You mean you still don't remember..."

"I know it was Booker," Anna repeated. "That's as clear to me as anything could be. When I heard him behind me in the dream, and I was afraid to turn to face him, I knew who it was, and I knew I was afraid to l¯ ʻ‹ at him. There's no question in my mind about it. The full memory is going to come to me at any moment. That's why I wanted to talk about it. I think I can bring it back. I'm very close now, very close. But what'll I do when I'm sure, when I know everything?''

"Call the police. Did you seriously think of not telling them?''

"No...not really...yes, of course, I have to tell the police.''

"You always were free of that fuzzy liberal guilt that makes some people regard mugging as one of the rights of the disaffected. And, remember, next time he might do a better job. Especially if it wasn't a mugging.'' Arno hesitated as if he did not want to say something that would alarm her, frighten her still more.

"You mean if he...really were just after me. Revenge. Do you think...''

Arno shrugged, sat still for a moment, then shook his head. "Doesn't sound like something a guy would do three years later.''

"There's something else.'' Anna decided it was time to tell him about the strange note she had received.

He listened with the same stillness. "You'd think if it was Booker, he'd have sent the note sooner, before he attacked you. Before or after...I don't know. It doesn't make much sense...three years after your trouble with him.''

"Unless he's more...his anger has grown since he left school... with nothing to look forward to, feeling betrayed...with hatred...''

"Can't rule out that possibility,'' Arno sighed.

"Maybe I should call that policeman...''

"And tell him you had a dream?'' Arno laughed, an exasperated sound. He leaned back and shook his head at her.

Anna responded the way she used to when he looked at her with tolerant amusement: she blushed.

His smile broadened. "So, she's still there, that girl, even if I haven't seen her for a long time.'' He leaned forward and took her hand. "Not for a long time. I've been worried about you these last couple of years. You haven't been yourself.''

"What's that supposed to mean?'' Anna could feel her blush deepening with her annoyance.

"Staying up here all day, doing God knows what. Never even heard you moving about. Once in a while I'd hear the rocker creak. Is that what you were doing, sitting by the window like a senile old crone in

132

one of those homes?''

Anna did not answer.

"And the nocturnal business. Leaving the house at all hours, and when I warned you about it, creeping out so I wouldn't hear you.''

"I had trouble sleeping.''

"Sure, because you sat around here all day. And then crept out at night. What did you do? Where did you go?''

"I don't know. I just...walked.''

"You always walked...miles, I guess...but in daylight, and going somewhere.'' Arno stopped and looked unhappy, almost sullen, complaining. "But the worst thing was, I couldn't talk to you anymore. You were always the one person in the world I could talk to. But I couldn't anymore.''

"Why not?'' Anna tried to remember conversations of the past two years. She could not remember doing anything but listening to Arno as she always had.

"You seemed to look through me, as if I weren't there. I'll tell you, Anna, your look is normally something to contend with, when those eyes make connection...but when they don't connect at all, when they look right through a man...''

"I don't know what you mean. I'm looking at you now. Am I looking through you?''

She was standing above him. He held onto her hand, making her incline slightly toward him. He looked up into her eyes and shook his head. "No, you're looking right at me again. Like the old Anna again. Yes, like that, by God. The first time I saw you, I said to myself, now that girl grabs hold of reality and won't let go no matter how it twists and changes. That's the woman to bounce your words against, to see if they ring clear or fall with a thud. That's what I missed in you these last couple of years. And since...whatever happened to you...it's back again. I could fall in love with you all over again.''

Anna gently pulled her hand back and crossed the room, leaving Arno looking up uncertainly, his hand still held out toward her. She reached the window, then turned back and looked around the room. "What a lot of junk there is in this place. I'm surprised you can move about. I must get rid of Mama's things, everything.''

As she walked to the door, Arno watched her intently. He opened his mouth to speak, then hesitated, then tried again. "I...wouldn't do anything too hasty.''

She looked back, surprised, as she opened the door. "Why, I think that's the first time I ever heard you say that." It was only as she moved through the doorway that she realized something had happened between them. For the first time in fifty years, he had reached out to her and she had sidestepped beyond his reach. It had taken no effort, no opposing of will against need. She had not thought about it or planned it or even wanted it. It simply was, now. Something was finally over.

She went outside to pick up the mail. The sun was bright and warm, and the air buzzed with insect sounds above the traffic sounds below. Everything, the sun, the noises, blended in a warm, alive throbbing that both soothed her and energized her. What a fine day for a walk!

Then she heard a shrill screaming from the street below. Lydia stood in her front garden, holding a large purple ball in her hands, yelling. In the street, three boys stood very still, waiting for her to finish yelling and give back the ball. She pointed to her flowers. The boys waited. Once, they had yelled back at her, and she had refused to return their ball. That quarrel took days of negotiation with their parents before it was resolved. Lydia, Anna thought, enjoyed every hateful moment of it.

Anna turned quickly and went into the house before Lydia might see her. She felt as if Lydia were the carrier of a contagious disease to which old people were especially susceptible, and, while she pitied her, she dare not expose herself again.

She opened the mail on the way upstairs, sighing with relief: no crank scrawls. There were two ads, a petition to increase police gun power, and an invitation to join something called Senior Singles, a dating service for people over fifty. And three more letters from former students. She read their names, clear and familiar on the envelopes. How amazing that they. . . cared about her. She would read them later when her mind was not so preoccupied, when she could savor their kindness.

She sat down in the rocking chair, looking out the window, trying to remember. She rocked jerkily back and forth, then stopped. The rocking chair was a place of no thought, of teetering over nothing. She got up from it quickly, thinking that she must get rid of that chair. It was all right for her mother. Rocking meant something different to her. But rocking was never any good for Anna.

She paced up and down the room, then through the other rooms. The movement did not help either, did not jog her memory. She was distracted by the things she saw as she paced around the apartment:

134

this must go, why had she kept that? What a strange place this had become, full of things she no longer had any use for. How could she think straight in such a place?

The key to her memory was Booker Henderson. She could visualize him plainly. Tall, thin, deeply black, black as the night sky, a well-shaped head with hair cropped close, features broadly Negroid. A strikingly handsome boy, clear-eyed, intense. Her glance had been drawn to his beauty almost as it had once been drawn to Stephen's. Did he know he was handsome? Obviously not, and all the slogans in the world could not have convinced him he was. He stood erect, but stiff. His look was searching, but frightened, hostile, inviting attack, demanding it, refusing to accept anything else, so that he could stay as he was, stiff and angry and untried. And afraid. Mostly afraid.

She concentrated on the image until she wore it out, blurred it. She was unable to call it up any longer, and she had gained nothing by it, not a glimpse of herself with him. She tried to imagine him in the dark, on the street, but her imagination quit on her. Her mind was blank.

Then an absurd idea filled it: if she could not hold him in her imagination, why shouldn't she try to find him, the real Booker, in the flesh? She could call the school, which would have some record of his address, his phone. Of course, it would be an outdated one; Camino High students were like migratory birds, their families moving constantly through narrowly prescribed areas.

She went to the back room, to her desk, and picked up the phone. Then she stopped. It was Saturday, and there would be no one at the school or even at the central office. She saw the telephone book on the edge of the desk. She sat down.

There was a half-page of Hendersons in the book. It would take a long time to call all of them, but she had time. She had more time than she had ever had, now that she was nearing the end of her life, and time was short. And she had had a lifetime of methodical persistence.

"Is this the home of Booker Henderson, formerly a student at Camino Real High School?"

It was like walking into strange homes, one after another, in rapid succession. She could tell a white household the moment she heard the voice, but mechanically repeated her question anyway. Sometimes there was music in the background, sometimes voices. Sometimes the answering voice was cold, sometimes it sounded sleepy, other times hopeful and then irritated, as if the ring of the telephone promised something Anna failed to deliver. Some asked her to repeat the question two or three times, as if they were deaf to any words they had not expected to hear.

"Is this the home of Booker Henderson, formerly a student at Camino Real High School?" There was a long pause. Anna waited for the low, tired woman's voice. She heard breathing. "I'm trying to locate Booker Henderson." She waited again.

"Who's this?"

"My name is Anna Giardino. I used to be a teacher at Camino Real High School. Booker was one of my students."

"You a teacher?" The slow, suspicious, stupid-sounding demand for repetition was familiar to Anna. It was the playing for time by chronically frightened people. Her father used to do the same thing, pretending that he did not understand English very well.

"Yes. I was Booker's teacher at Camino." Then she took a chance and leaped ahead. "Is he there?"

"No."

"But he does live there?"

Again the pause, then the slow, suspicious voice. "What you want him for?"

It was Anna's turn to hesitate. She had not thought this far ahead. She had not planned what she would say if she actually found him. Did he attack me last Sunday night? "Are you his mother?" Now Anna was the one who was playing for time.

A long pause. "Yes." Silence. "He drop out of school two, three years ago. So he not the one you looking for."

"Yes, he is. He's the one."

"What you want with him?"

"I . . . I just wanted to know how he was getting on. I thought he . . . shouldn't have dropped out when he did. Lately I've been thinking of him . . . wondering how he was doing. . . ." It all sounded so improbable that Anna could not think she had convinced the woman even for a moment. In the silence that followed, she waited for the woman to hang up on her. But she heard only breathing.

"You . . . you that English teacher."

"Yes." That would finish it. The woman knew about her, knew about the old-maid-racist teacher. Anna waited again for the woman to hang up on her. Again she heard breathing. But this time the breathing suddenly caught in a choking sob.

"I don't know where he is. Haven't seen him since Sunday. Every time the phone ring I think it might be him . . . or . . . maybe it be about

136

him."

"You're afraid he's in trouble."

"Ever since he quit school, he do nothing but hang around, the Lord knows where, out all night sometime. I can't do nothing. I'm working. How can I watch him all the time? He sleep in the daytime and go out before I come home from work. Sometime I lay awake trying to hear him come in. But I got to sleep. I got other children, I go to work early, I just can't..."

"He's never stayed away this long before?"

"He always home in a few hours. Where else can he go? What can he do? You know how he was in school? Worse, now, nothing to do and going with some bad people. I used to tell him, that old teacher, she sound like your grandma; she used to scold and worry us children and even beat us with a stick, but only to make us do right."

"You did?" The woman had actually defended her! There had been someone on her side. If she had known that, would it have made any difference? Probably not.

"But he won't listen," the woman went on. "I try to tell him, there's chances for him I never had. But he don't want to hear. I don't know what he want. I say to him, that old teacher just telling you how to read and write, that's all. You go in there and learn. Don't matter she's white or black. Don't matter if she don't like you, if she willing to teach you something. But he won't listen."

"What kind of trouble do you think he might be in?" Anna asked cautiously.

The woman hesitated, then it seemed as if she decided to trust Anna. "I'm afraid...afraid he did something."

"Sunday night?"

"Um...he did something and afraid of getting caught. Afraid to come home. Every time the phone ring or the doorbell I think maybe it's the police. That's why when you called..."

Anna was exhilarated. It all fit. Booker knew she had recognized him. That was why he had run away without taking anything. She shuddered. In his fear of being recognized and reported to the police, he might have killed her. But he didn't. He didn't. He simply ran away and hid.

"Well, maybe he'll be lucky this time. Maybe it wasn't as serious as he thought. Maybe after a few days he'll call you and know it's safe, and he'll come back."

"I almost hope he don't. He just come back to the same life again,

137

the same bad people. I wish he start going and just keep going, even if I never see him again, just so he break loose from this life he been living..."

"Then maybe it was a good thing. I mean, if something frightened him."

"Maybe. He just a boy. Wild, but if he just get to be twenty, twenty-one, start to settle down a little. Sometime that all it takes, just time."

"Then let's hope he's far away, and safe," said Anna. "Let's hope he stays frightened long enough to stay out of trouble for a while. Let's hope..."

Anna heard a child wail.

"I got to go now. If he come back I'll tell him you called."

Anna smiled as she hung up, wondering how Booker would react if he were told she had called.

She leaned back in her chair and gave a great sigh of relief. Through the window she saw that the old plum tree in the back of the house was blooming. Since the boxes had been removed from her desk, she could see through this window for the first time since she retired. She sighed again, as if a great burden had fallen away. Booker had not intended to harm her. The possibility of a hate-ridden student, stalking her as she walked at night, and finally attacking her, was gone, need not be considered. Booker had not written the crank note. She now dismissed the note entirely. It meant nothing. Booker was innocent. He might have tried to mug her, but he was innocent, she thought irrationally, and she was free of her worst fear.

She even thought she had a fleeting, shadowy memory of a grab at her purse. As soon as she tried to examine the memory, it dissolved, but not before giving her thoughts direction. Booker had simply tried to steal her purse, had been recognized and, dropping the purse, had run away. But that did not explain Anna's fall. Could she just have slipped?

She closed her eyes, trying to visualize herself and Booker. She could create the images and put them through various scenarios of what might have happened. But she still had no genuine memory. Her head began to ache from trying so hard. And she realized she was hungry. She looked at the clock on her desk. It was after six. The whole day was gone.

She opened a can of soup, warmed it slowly, and ate it with a few crackers. She wondered if when she fell asleep tonight her dream would complete the story for her, finally giving her the total memory.

138

She doubted it. Dreams were useful when they moved ahead of consciousness, but her conscious mind had now moved ahead of her dreams. Hints and symbols would not connect with total conscious memory. Trying to remember only sealed tight the door between her and the facts she knew but did not know. The right lever, tripped, would open the door. But where was that lever?

She laughed. The return to the scene of the crime. Wasn't that what all the old detective stories did? The re-enactment. Anna had always said that her dozens of mystery story books were the only ones from which she did not expect to learn anything, but now, chuckling, she decided she had been mistaken.

She looked out the window, watching blossoms fall in the stiff wind that had come up. There would be no fog tonight, but the spring wind that blew it away would be cold. It would not be dark for another hour.

She washed the dishes and put them away. Then she went to the front room, sat down in the rocking chair and watched the sky darken. Wasn't that what she had done every day? Yes, she had sat there for a long time.

And then what did she do? She went to bed, of course. Anna got up and walked to her bedroom. She went carefully through the whole ritual, undressing, brushing her teeth, carefully brushing her hair, aware of how much came out in the brush and how little of it would be replaced now. Then she went to bed and lay in the dark. She remembered how she would lie in the dark waiting for sleep that did not come. She would lie there for hours, until the clock passed one or two and her body ached all over no matter which way she turned, and she would have to get up.

It was still early, but there was no need to make the re-enactment too literal. After lying there for half an hour, she got up. She tried to make her motions automatic, tried to split her mind into two parts, the automatic part which followed the habitual motions, and the distant, objective, rational part, the witness that watched without interfering. She took off her pajamas, put on her underwear and the dark wool pants and shirt she had worn Sunday night. She went to the closet for her shoes and her old coat. She picked up her purse and was ready to go. But at the door, she stopped, feeling as if she had forgotten something. She could not remember what. Her witness made note of a possible omission. Then she opened the door.

Until then she had gone through the motions casually, almost lightheartedly, but as she opened her door, a wave of dread swept through her, hitting her like an icy wind, chilling her. She had to force herself to put one foot in front of the other, stepping slowly down the dark stairway, afraid of attracting Arno's attention if she turned on the light. Her knees felt so weak that she clutched the bannister with both hands. Her silent witness watched, merely noting that she was terrified, more terrified than she had ever been of anything in her life.

As she reached the big front door, she whispered, "I am not, and never have been, afraid of the dark."

Out on the porch, feeling her way down the steps to the garden she said, "I am not afraid of being attacked again."

Creeping down the sloping stone steps to the street, she said, "I am afraid of remembering. I am afraid of a memory, a shadow, an image in the back of my mind. I will be afraid until I remember. Then it'll be gone, like a pulled tooth."

She set her jaw, turned to the right and walked to the end of the block. Then she turned left, starting downhill on her familiar route, the way she had walked down to school every day as a student, then as a teacher, and then...late at night, in the dark, when she should have been asleep.

The witness part of her mind now became a goad, driving her on, forcing her to put one foot before the other. Her fear did not abate. With every step it grew, until she had a new fear, that her terror might make her heart stop. An old heart like hers surely could not be forced to pound and pound in this way without tearing itself apart. And if it did, said her strict witness, would it matter so much? You've lived as long as most people do, longer than many. If you are so afraid of something, hadn't you better know what it is?

She nagged and nagged at herself, not making her knees firmer or her heart calmer, but managing to keep her feet moving, one after the other, left, right, left, right, not letting herself look at the row of palm trees bisecting the street, afraid that even the familiar, squatty trunks and sloping fronds would change into menacing shapes. The street was empty. The wind had died. The air was still and cold. She crossed the park, cutting diagonally across the wet grass, the school in full view now, lit by an orangy full moon, gradually rising, shrinking, paling.

She stopped across the street from the school, standing on the pavement, the park behind her. She looked across the street to the broad stairs, the huge front door. She could not move another step. What words her rational mind might have attempted were drowned out by the pounding of her heart and by a queer rushing sound in her head, as if an amplifier had been turned up and she heard a thousand city noises blurred into one great roar.

She stood without the courage to move or to think. She believed she would soon faint and die. She accepted the possibility without courage or defiance, but with simple, humiliating acknowledgement of her helplessness, and with an even simpler wish that she could understand what it was that seemed to be frightening her to death.

She dug her freezing hands into her pockets. Each of them closed over foreign objects, strange, confusing objects. She drew her hands out of her pockets and looked at them. In her left hand she held a key. In her right hand she held five matches.

It started in her hands, where the key and the matches touched her palms. It started like an electric current. Memory charged through her body like an electric charge, and she cried out with the shock and the pain.

The high, chirping voice nagged at her. "Miss Giardino. Are you all right? Miss Giardino, it's Lori. We were just driving home and saw you...won't you let us take you home? Come on, Lorenzo, let's get her up off the curb. You take that side. Miss Giardino, can you stand up? That's it, good. I guess you went out for a walk and got tired, so you just sat down on the curb. God, she's freezing. She must have been here for...here you go, that's it. I'll get in back with her."

Anna felt the motion of the car, felt her hands being held and rubbed, heard Lori's voice chattering on, sometimes making sense, sometimes only drowning out Anna's own thoughts. If only Lori would keep still. Yet, Anna was glad to see her, grateful. She could not have made it up the hill, not without time to recover, and it was probable that she could not recover very well, sitting out on that cold curb, where she had dropped like a rag doll when the terror let go and cold, cruel consciousness flooded in to take its place.

She shook her head and put her finger to her lips. "Sh..." She realized how foolish the gesture looked and sounded, but it made Lori quiet for a moment, still holding Anna's hands, while Anna's mind raced and words tried to rush out. But her mind was working again and held back the words. Not now, not here, no confessions. Let them get your body home. Then take time to decide what to do with what you know.

141

"I'm all right now," Anna said. "Yes, I went for a walk. That was silly. I wasn't strong enough yet. I felt a little faint and sat down on the curb to wait until it passed."

"Can you make it up the steps?"

"Yes. I'll just lean on your arm. There."

"Slowly now. Don't rush."

"I'll be fine, as soon as I get inside where it's warm."

They insisted on following her into her apartment and making her a cup of tea. She drank it obediently, trying to hurry, burning her tongue as she took quick gulps. The tea helped to warm her, and if she finished it quickly she could make them go. They had to go, so that she could think.

A door closed downstairs and footsteps came, faster than might be expected, up the stairs. An impatient knock rattled the door.

"That'll be Arno," sighed Anna.

"What's going on?" he asked as Lori opened the door to let him in.

Then all three of them stood over her as she sat in the rocking chair, all disapproving, as annoyed as they would be at a disobedient child.

"You may go now," said Anna. "Arno will stay with me for a few minutes. Thank you. Thank you very much."

As soon as they were gone, Arno exploded. "Good Christ, Anna, what kind of senile tricks are you up to!"

"I thought if I retraced my steps, I'd remember."

"Of all the...." He stopped, looking at her face. "And did you?" He eased himself down onto the chair opposite her, folded his arms, and waited.

"I went walking down to the school. I used to walk down there, late at night, the way I did every morning when I was still teaching. Sometimes I'd forget I wasn't teaching any more, even forget it was dark, and when I got there and stood in front of the building, and saw it was empty and dark, and there was no reason to go there anymore...I'd stand there for a long time, I guess, and then I'd come home.

"Yes. Yes, I remembered. It was almost three o'clock. Empty streets. Not even a car had passed for a long time. I picked that time to be sure...." Here Anna hesitated. She felt herself beginning to tremble. No, she could not tell that part, not yet.

"I didn't see or hear Booker. He came up behind me. I just felt the grab at my purse. But my grip on it was stronger than he expected. Instead of the purse being pulled out of my hand...it was looped over my arm and my hand was in my pocket...." Anna's hands were in her pockets now, touching the evidence, the trigger of memory, the tangible signs. "Instead of pulling the purse away from me, he pulled me around to face him. We looked right into each other's faces, just inches apart." Almost nose to nose, they had looked at each other and recognized each other. She had seen his face freeze into shock at recognizing hers, just as her face froze.

"And then what? He knocked you down, and..."

"No." Anna shook her head. "Not quite. Not yet." She looked at Arno's face, then down to her lap. "I flew at him," she said softly. "I swung my purse at him. I clawed at his face. I was trying to get at his throat. I wanted to kill him. He must have been so surprised, he slipped and went down on one knee. I pounded his head with my fists. I kicked him. I..."

Arno burst out laughing. "By God, I wish I'd seen that. Anna, there's no one like you. I'd like to..."

Anna shook her head. "You don't understand. It wasn't that I was angry because he tried to rob me. I wasn't even thinking of that. It was because I recognized him. It was because I hated him so. Or not really him. He was everything I hated, everything that had gone wrong, everything about the school, about my life, everything I hated was... Booker. I hated him the way he hated me when I was his teacher. I was ...insane with hate."

"Go on."

"He got up. And he pushed me away. Just to get me off. Self-defense. He pushed me. I suppose I hit my head on the steps when I fell."

"Stop shaking, for Christ's sake. It's all over. You have remembered it, now you can forget it. After you call the police and tell them who it was."

"You don't understand," said Anna.

"I understand perfectly. You'd have knocked his brains out if you had the strength. But you didn't. That doesn't excuse what he did. I call it a good job. Insane? Who hasn't been in a rage sometime? You tell the police the whole story, including the few good punches you got in, and you'll be heroine of the year, Miss Super-senior-citizen."

Anna shook her head. "Not if I tell them everything." Anna drew her hands out of her pockets, and opened them palm upward on her lap. In one hand lay the key, in the other, the matches. She held them and looked at them just as she had when she stood in front of the school. "We're supposed to turn in all keys when we retire. But they didn't know I had that one. I got it years ago from a janitor who got tired of letting me in early. It's a master key, opens everything." She looked at Arno. "My plan was to get turpentine from the art room, splash it on the curtain in the auditorium, then open the doors on all three balconies, to let the fire spread throughout the building."

Silence.

Finally Arno rubbed his moustache, pursed his lips and said, "Amateurish. Heavy old curtain like that would probably fall and smother the flames."

"Don't you understand what I'm saying?"

"I understand. That's what you wanted to do. Hell, I've plotted worse. But you didn't do it."

"Only because he stopped me, Booker stopped me and I turned all of my...turned all of it on him."

"Bullshit. You'd never have done it. You thought it and wished it, but you never would have..."

"How do you know? Didn't you say I hadn't been myself for a long time? How do we know what I would have done?"

Arno shrugged. "We know you didn't, so..." He shrugged again. "...unless you want to try it again soon, do you?"

"Of course not, do you think I'm..." Crazy. Yet, it had seemed quite logical. It was the institution itself, the conditions, The System, as Arno always put it, that was to blame. Not her or the students or even the teachers she most despised. To remove, to obliterate one structure of that system seemed like the only way to force a change. Logical. It still seemed logical in a crazy sort of way.

"I went after my wife with a gun...twice," said Arno. "We're all crazy, but not usually enough to pull the trigger or strike the match. The ones who do, the ones who end up on the front page of the newspaper, well...they're not us, that's all. Forget it, Anna."

Anna shook her head. Arno would be of no help. He was too practiced at forgetting unpleasant things he did. Arno was always starting again, with a clean slate.

"I'm all right now," she said. "You may go."

"I'll stay as long as you need me." But already he was on his feet, yawning and moving toward the door. The act contradicting the word was so typical of Arno that Anna had to smile.

"That's more like it," he said, misunderstanding the smile. "It's all over now, and take my word for it, you and your young friend are just so much the better for it. You got forty years of frustration off your

144

chest, and he got a lesson that'll make him think twice before the next purse-snatching he tries. If it'll make you feel any better, don't report him to the police. Call it even-steven. Shook you out of the dumps and shook him up. You did him a favor. And he certainly did you one. You're both better off."

Yes. Exactly. Anna sat still in the silence after Arno left. Now what should she do?

She could go to the police and tell them she was an arsonist, accidentally stopped from setting fire to the school. She could show them the key and the matches, and they would doubtless give her a pat on the head and send her home. But they would surely go after Booker, and they would not give him a pat on the head.

She could go to a doctor and ask to be put away somewhere in a place where they kept people who lost their minds. She had misplaced her mind, and had found it again. Might she not misplace it again and not locate it in time, next time? Or not have it thrust back at her, as Booker had done, pushing her back into her mind?

She tried to put the question rationally: what should be done with an old woman capable of attempting to burn down a school in order to relieve her pent-up fury? She had no answer. She could not even imagine such an old woman. She could not imagine how such a mind worked, how it could reach such a conclusion. She had come back from where she was, from a place reached only by being so thoroughly lost that she did not know where she had been or how she had gotten there.

She knew only that she had been brought back, accidentally and unintentionally brought back, by Booker. He had interrupted her and had taken the full force of her stored up anger, just as she had, over the years, received the accumulation of injury and frustration, ignorance and fear, from so many young people. Madness piles up, fills you up, and must be let out. Was it as simple as that? Released madness makes others mad, and they too, must let it break out. Simple. An exchange of fury, endlessly repeated, the history of human life, the trading of destruction. What was there to be learned from this? That no one was exempt? That there was no way of stopping the futile and destructive exchange? Like the endless exchange of matter in nature, life forms merging into one another, eating one another in the ceaseless violence of energy exchange, human feeling and energy was transformed into violent bursts people vented upon one another.

Anna thought again of her father. In her mind, she saw him,

gasping and shaking his fist at God. He had made the great effort to change life, to bring hope to it. He had endured the horrible wrench of the emigrant, out of misery to desperate hope. But all hope had been eroded away until only desperation was left.

And how had she differed from her father? At first she had hated him; then she forgot him. Now, finally, she understood him. She had learned to understand him by becoming him. He had a vision of a better life and had strained himself to the utmost to go after it. So had she. He had been used and abused by the forces in which he had put all his hope. So had she. He had become filled with hatred and bitterness and despair, and had vented his hatred on the nearest targets. So, finally, had she.

Anna could barely get up from the rocking chair. She made it to the bedroom, keeping her fingertips on the walls, like a drunk trying to steady herself. She stepped out of her shoes, dropping her clothes on the floor, and let herself down on the bed. It took all her strength to pull the blankets up over her. The weight of them seemed enough to crush her. Maybe now she would die. Enough had happened, more than enough in the past few days, to kill an old woman. This exhaustion might be the beginning of dying.

As she sank toward sleep, one last dim thought of her father drifted through her mind. There was one difference between them. It was a difference in what they knew. Arno was wrong. She must not forget what she now knew about herself. If she forgot, if she dulled her consciousness, she would die in the same despair as her father, without even his hope of a new generation to benefit from his sacrifice.

SUNDAY

DAVID KNOCKED FOR THE third time. He stood uncertainly, his plump hand half raised to knock again. Then he turned toward the stairway.

He hesitated, then walked quickly down the stairs and knocked on Arno's door. After a long time, the door was pulled open and Arno stood frowning at him, wearing a wrinkled robe over dark pants. For a moment they looked at each other in silence.

"Is Anna here?"

Arno shook his head and started to close the door.

"I wouldn't bother you, but there's no answer upstairs, and she was expecting me. Could she be sleeping this late or did she go out?"

Arno shook his head. "I heard her walking around up there early this morning. I usually hear her if she comes down the stairs." He turned away.

"You don't think," said David, "she might be ill."

Arno stopped, stood still for a moment, then turned around slowly to look at David.

"Is there. . . something?"

"I don't know," said Arno. "She was a bit off color last night. But she looked all right when I left her." Arno shrugged. "Oh, Anna's a sensible girl; she must be all right."

"But something did happen last night. . . she was upset?" When Arno didn't answer, David took a deep breath. "I hate to suggest anything so dramatic as breaking down a door, but don't you think we'd better check to make sure she's all right?"

Arno threw back his head and laughed. Then he looked at David, rubbing his moustache as if it had tickled him into laughter. "Pardon me, but I just had a sudden flash of us breaking down the door and rushing to the rescue. I'm not the man I used to be, and you never were."

147

David waited.

"All right, all right. No need to break it down. My key opens it." He waited to enjoy David's expression before explaining that the two doors were keyed the same for Anna and her mother, and she had never bothered to change the locks.

Arno led the way up the stairs, groaning several times before reaching the top. He insisted that David knock again before he inserted the key, swung the door wide, walked in, and sharply called, "Anna!"

There was no response.

They went straight to the bedroom. She was not there. The bed was neatly made up. They glanced into her study and into the bathroom. "Well, damn it, where is she?" Arno muttered as he stood in the kitchen flexing his fingers and frowning.

"She must have gone out."

"I didn't think she'd do that again."

"Do what again?"

"Sneak out. So I wouldn't hear her. She did it last night...went out to visit the 'scene of the crime.' To help get her memory back. She got her memory back all right, damn near worked herself into a heart attack. Scared the living hell out of me."

"She remembered? What did she remember?"

"The whole thing. The mugging."

"It must have been very traumatic, like living through it all again."

"And then she had some fool idea that she was the criminal, instead of the guy who..." Arno walked into the dining room, David following.

"I don't understand. How could she be the criminal?"

The two men stood facing each other across the round oak table.

"Said she was on her way to burn down the school, and the mugger stopped her."

"She said what!"

"I just told you; you're not deaf, are you? And stop looking at me that way."

"And what did you do? What did you say to her?"

"Told her to forget it, what else was there to say? Not the first person who ever wanted to blow up something or burn it down, or... a big gap between the intention and the deed. I told her."

"And how did she respond?"

"Well, you know Anna. That wouldn't satisfy her."

"You shouldn't have left her alone."

148

"God damn it, don't tell me what I should or shouldn't...she's always been so sensible...except, no, last couple of years she's been...oh, Christ, she's probably in some police station making a confession."

"We could call the police," said David.

"And ask if some loony old woman arsonist is there?"

"I meant, just to report her missing." David's voice was almost a whisper, getting softer as Arno's grew louder.

Arno shook his head. "You don't report a person missing because she walked out of her apartment on a Sunday morning."

"No, I suppose we'll have to wait until she's been gone for a while."

"She couldn't have gone far."

"I could get into my car," said David, "and cruise the neighborhood."

Both men moved toward the front room. They stood at the window looking down. The morning fog was still thick. The park was barely visible, all greens smoky gray.

"It's not like Anna," said David, "to do anything irrational."

"It's not like anyone. But then they do it. We get old and our bodies betray us, our stinking bodies go to pieces, tormenting our minds." Arno was looking at his swollen fingers. "Until our minds go too. The final humiliation. Senility or stupidity. I'll probably go twirling down the street in a tutu one of these days soon. Though that might be more in your line."

David seemed not to hear. "I'll just go cruise the neighborhood," he said softly, "and perhaps you can wait in your apartment in case she calls."

As they walked down the stairway, they saw the young couple standing in front of Arno's open door.

"Oh, Mr. Steadman," said Lori, "we were just looking for you." Lori wore a long dress with a man's vest-sweater over it. She had cut off her long hair; it was so short it seemed plastered to her head. Lorenzo wore nothing but a pair of khaki shorts. His hair was pulled tightly back in a pony tail, his bald crown seeming even more naked than usual.

"I'm too busy to talk to you now," said Arno. "You haven't seen Miss Giardino, have you?"

"That's what we wanted to talk to you about," said Lori. "She left a message for you, and for..." She looked at the scrap of paper in her hand. "Mr. Stern...are you Mr. Stern?"

149

David nodded. "She told you where she was going?"

"Well, no, but she said to tell you she'd gone, and ..."

"Come inside," Arno ordered. "When did you see her, what did she say?"

They all followed Arno into his apartment. Lorenzo kept his usual silence, but looked around the front room as if taking inventory.

"Oh, look, Lorenzo, all those darling things her mother used to crochet. Why, we could open a store just with them!"

"The message!" said Arno. He and David sat on the sofa. Lori and Lorenzo immediately dropped to the floor and sat crosslegged; Lorenzo grimaced as he folded his legs.

"She said to tell you she'd call," said Lori. "We were supposed to tell you sooner, but we fell asleep again. Sorry."

"Is that all?"

"That's the message, yes."

"Didn't she say where she was going?"

Lori shook her head.

"That's all she said?" asked David. "She just said she would call, and then she left?"

"Oh, no, that's not all she said. We had a pretty long talk. What a strange morning!"

"What was strange? Was she...did she act strangely?"

"Miss Giardino? Oh, of course not. But it was strange the way she did it. I mean, she came to our place early this morning. She said she was sorry she woke us up, but she had come to a decision and wanted to settle everything and had to be going."

"Settle what?" asked David.

"The house. We've always wanted to own this house. I mean, the first time we saw it we wanted it, didn't we, Lorenzo." Lorenzo nodded. "But, of course, we didn't have any money until Lorenzo sold his book. He wrote a book on bumming, you know, living on nothing, and the paperback contract came yesterday, and now we won't have to live on nothing anymore." Lorenzo nodded.

"We already told Miss Giardino we had enough for a down payment. We knew what she'd say. She always said she would never sell this place, but we just told her in case she changed her mind... but she sure surprised us..."

"For God's sake, girl, get to the point," said Arno.

Lori smiled. "She said she had made up her mind to sell us the house on one condition, that we take it as is, with everything in it. She just couldn't think about moving and clearing things out and trying to decide what to keep and what to sell, and so on. She said she just wanted to walk away from it, and she was sure we'd reach a fair price and finish all the details later. Oh, and she said another condition was that we let you stay, Mr. Steadman, until you found something else." Lori smiled again, the polite but firm smile of a landlady.

"But where was she going?"

"She wasn't sure. She said she'd call you, not to worry; sometime today, she'd call so you could forward her mail."

"Tell me," said David, "what was her...state of mind? Did she seemed disturbed?"

"Oh, no," said Lori. "She was just the way she always is. Just ...Miss Giardino."

"And you just let her...." Arno was turning red.

"Thank you so much," said David, smoothly and quietly cutting Arno off. He stood up and smiled, nodding a gentle dismissal of the two young people. They immediately got to their feet and started for the door. As David closed the door behind them, he heard Lori say, "I've just got to go look at her books again. That'll be our library. We'll knock down all those partitions and...."

Arno shook his head sideways toward the door. "Two young vultures, expecting to cash in on someone else's insanity. They'll find they can't..."

"Insanity?" David stood near a tall, narrow table, fingering a pink, web-like doily. "You think Anna's mentally ill?"

"Not ill, just...not herself, that's obvious, not right now."

"Why, because she decided to sell the house?"

"You mean you don't see anything strange about all this?"

David shrugged. "She's had no reason to hang onto this place since her mother died. In fact, I advised her against buying it in the first place. Too near the school. I wanted her finally to get out of The Mission. But she said her mother had friends here and liked the sun, would be lonely and cold in the foggier parts of town."

"I think the old lady is the only person she ever really cared about," Arno complained. "So. It might make sense to sell the place, but like this? sneaking off without a word? leaving everything?"

David disagreed. "It might have been hard to do it any other way. To sort through all her belongings, to give up this, keep that. We all tend to cling too much to things, especially as we get older. So once she made up her mind..."

151

"God, you make me sick! If there were blood all over the floor you'd probably say it was a nice, red color. Here a woman who's had a blow on the head, memory loss, a rational, deliberate, reserved, absolutely predictable woman, suddenly walks off into nowhere and you're as unruffled as a God-damned imbecile."

David was silent for a moment. Then he answered, in a voice with just a slight edge to it, "You're not concerned about Anna, and you never have been. You're not afraid for her. You're incensed... because for the first time in her life, she's left you when it suited her, instead of the other way around." David's voice had remained soft, gotten softer, and was now silky smooth. "The only thing you're worried about is where you're going to go now that she's finally thrown you out!"

Arno's lips quivered slightly as he looked up to the ceiling, then lowered a bland gaze directly into David's eyes. "Been thinking about Mexico. Cuernavaca. Supposed to be a doctor there who does wonders for arthritis. Puts you on a diet of ground cherry pits or some damned thing."

The telephone rang. Both Arno and David turned toward where it sat, on a low stool at the end of the sofa. It rang three times before David looked at Arno, received a short nod, and picked up the receiver.

Arno got up and paced back and forth.

"Hello...yes, my dear, yes...yes, Lori told us. Where are you? May we come to talk to you? Yes...right...oh, I see...yes, see you in a moment. Good-bye." He turned to Arno as he hung up. "She's at forty-eight Phoenix. That's just down the street."

"Just down the street?" Arno frowned, then nodded. "The place with the new paint job. Yellow. What's she doing there? Is she coming back here?"

David shook his head. "She says she's rented a room there."

"Now if that isn't...woman leaves her home and rents a room on the same block." Arno opened his mouth again, then gave up and shrugged silently, wincing as he sank back down on the couch.

David took a step toward the door. "Coming?"

Arno leaned back and shook his head. "I feel rotten. Take me a while just to get some clothes on. Besides, when that woman makes up her mind to do something, there's not a thing you can do."

152

Anna stood at the window, looking down...down to the fog-wet sidewalk where David frowned up at the stairs as if counting them. He hesitated, then started the long climb. Anna smiled. There were more stairs than at her house, criss-crossing the steeply terraced front garden. Poor David would be out of breath. Slowly, David. Take it easy.

She crossed the room, opened the door and went out to the stair landing. From there she could see down the stairs to the front door. The bell rang, and Anna smiled again. It was a deep, oriental gong whose brassy vibrations died slowly, and she almost giggled when she thought of David's reaction to setting off such exotic echoes with the touch of his finger.

The landlady opened the door, shoving back a drop cloth with one foot and wiping one hand on her overalls. From the back, Anna could not see what she held in the other hand; it looked like a trowel.

"...last time I heard a sound like that was in Tibet in, let's see, 1947?" said David's voice, followed by the woman's pleased giggle. "Miss Giardino, please."

"Oh, sure, she's in the room right at the top of the stairs. I'd let you use the living room, but it's all over plaster. Watch your step." She backed up, and David moved into visibility.

Anna called, "Come right up, David." She watched him make the final climb, panting and looking up at her. At first his look was anxious, but as he came nearer he began smiling, looking relieved.

"Ah, isn't that..."

"Yes, the sweater you brought me from Alaska."

"Charming with those blue pants."

"Thank you. Are you alone?"

"Arno wasn't feeling well."

"How did he react to...the change?"

"He's talking about going to Mexico," said David, raising his eyebrows.

Anna smiled. For once it seemed funny that Arno always had somewhere else to go.

David followed Anna into her room, and she watched him taking in the long window, the small round table before it, cluttered with the letters Anna was beginning to answer, the one straight chair, the narrow bed where Anna's coat and purse lay. "Bare walls," he murmured. "No curtains to block your view."

"She just finished painting this room."

153

"Um. Rather like a cell. Monastic, I mean."

Anna nodded. "Yes, right down to essentials." The thought was a warm wave of satisfaction. She pointed to the chair, and David sat down on it. She sat on the bed.

"I was a bit worried about you, my dear," said David, looking at her intently, "But I must say..." He shook his head, puzzled. "...you look radiant."

"Yes. I had a wonderful night's sleep. Slept like the dead, as they say. I..." It had been like a death, but she didn't know how to describe it to David, nor how to describe the way she awoke, feeling so different, so new. "I haven't slept like that in years."

"And, it seems, you made some decisions."

"Yes."

"Rather sudden decisions."

"Some decisions have to be made suddenly if they're to be made at all." Anna made a sweeping motion with her hands, then noticed that David watched every move like a doctor alert to signs of illness... mental illness. She dropped her hands into her lap. "I'm selling the house to Lori and Lorenzo. This room is promised to someone else in three months, but I can stay here that long. And then...I don't know."

David smiled. "At least you'll finally be getting out of The Mission."

Anna started to nod, then shrugged uncertainly. "Did you know that your father's old dry-goods store is a bookstore? And the shop my family lived over is now called the Chicano Culture Center? I've been meaning to drop in there and see..." David started to nod politely, then looked puzzled and alert again. "I'm not sure 'getting out of The Mission' means the same thing it used to. If I leave now, won't I miss...what's happening here?" Poor David had no idea what she meant. She wasn't sure she knew herself. And, anyway, it didn't matter whether she did or not.

"I certainly approve of your finally selling that old house," said David. "I don't understand this fad for fixing up old relics, especially among these young people. You'd think they'd want to tear down the old and build new." David tapped the floor with one foot. "They'll never get rid of the smell of rotting timbers no matter what they do."

Anna nodded.

"I just wondered...about something Arno said."

"What did Arno tell you?" Anna knew the answer, and she was ready.

David looked out the window. "He said something about...about

154

your wishing you could burn down the school."

"Not wishing, David, intending. I took my old master key and several matches, intending to burn down the place. I had rather a good, simple plan. I was..."

"Now, now, of course. We all make plans like that. But the plan and the deed are two quite different things, aren't they? You thought about it, and you walked down there, but chances are you just would have walked past, the way you always did."

"I don't know. I was stopped before I reached that point."

"Anna, you mustn't brood on things like this. We all have... moments when we think of things we wouldn't do, not really, and it's best to forget those moments as soon as they're past, not to dwell on ...our darker moments."

"David, last night, as I was going to sleep, I realized how very much like my father I am. How much like his life my life became."

"Oh, come now, you're not like him at all!"

"He struggled to get out of an intolerable life in the Old Country. But nothing ever really changed. He was defeated by the new country he came to. I struggled too..."

"But you were not defeated."

"Wasn't I? I don't know. I felt defeated, when I retired. And angry. Mad. I think of all the years when I used to correct papers, marking 'wrong word' in the margin when my students used 'mad' to mean 'angry'. But they were right. Anger is a kind of madness. My father was mad with anger. So was I."

"Never! You exaggerate. You have always been rational and consistent, except..."

"Except now?" Anna smiled as the anxiety took over David's face again.

"You're still rational. It's quite rational to get rid of that old house, but I don't...I don't like this...this talk about your father...and madness...and brooding over the past..."

Anna shook her head. "Not brooding, not..." How could she convince him that she was not dwelling on the past but only going through it, finally, finally passing through it. "I'm through with the past, but I mustn't lose it. What I mean is..." It was hopeless. "You agree that my decision to leave the house was a good one."

"Absolutely. I like the way you did it. Courageously. Just walking away. That was necessary. Otherwise you would spend months, maybe years, agonizing over what to take. Now you can give me a list

155

of things you want, and I'll go back and. . ."

Anna shook her head. "I have identification, bank book and tooth-brush in my purse." She had mailed the key to the school, but carried in her purse one match, carefully struck and blown out, as a reminder.

"But you'll need some clothes."

"Tomorrow I'll buy a change of clothes, to wear while I wash these."

"But surely you'll. . ."

"If I need anything else, I'll buy it new."

David's eyes lit up. "Oh, yes, a new wardrobe for a new life. Of course, Anna. You've never indulged yourself. All the years I've known you, it's been a few sensible dresses and a few sensible shoes, but now. . ."

Anna smiled. He thought she would buy a wardrobe of elegant clothes instead of another pair of pants and sweater. He didn't understand. No matter. She felt no need to explain.

"And what about your books?"

"The libraries are full of books."

"You mother's things? Perhaps just one memento. . .a photograph, one of the handkerchiefs she edged. . ."

Anna nodded. "I must call my sister. . .see if she wants anything. But I don't need anything to help me remember Mama. I want to travel light, strip down to essentials."

"When did you start to feel this way?"

"Last week, when I was talking to a neighbor. Suddenly I was afraid I had become like her, clinging to old things, hating people as if they would rob her of her things, screaming at children who so much as broke a blade of grass in her front garden."

David shrugged. "That's how we get, I suppose."

"I won't live that way." Or die that way.

"You always were defiant, my dear, always refusing the usual patterns of living. So you renounce it all."

"Yes, that's what we should do as we get old. Let go of it all." Anna wondered if she could communicate the excitement of it to David. "Be free. No belongings. Like a child again, but better than childhood because we know some things now. Independent. Cut loose from responsibility."

David's smile was patient but dubious. "But you know very well, my dear, that is exactly what is so frightening about growing old."

"Frightening things aren't always bad for you."

156

"You admit what you're doing frightens you."

"Yes." Anna felt her jaw tightening. "If I were young it would be different. It's risky, being young. The young have to live a whole lifetime with their mistakes. They should be cautious. But when we're old, there might be something to gain, and little to lose, if we gamble." Anna felt lifted, lightened by an unexpected idea. "Do you suppose that's what my sister really means when she goes to Reno and stands in front of those slot machines?" A laugh shook her jaw, loosened it again.

David jumped up from his chair and hugged her as he had done when he was a child and she, the solemn old thirteen year old, watched him play or sing or let him teach her the multiplication table. Only now, Anna thought, he seemed the older one. "You are wonderful, Anna, wonderful." He went down on one knee beside her. "Now that you are finally running away from home, why not run all the way?"

"What do you mean?"

"To the south of France. I have friends there. They'll be your friends too. We'll find a little villa for you. We'll take trips. I'll show you Europe."

"David, I hate travel."

"All right, then you can stay put. It will be a quiet, comfortable life, with a few civilized acquaintances, far away from this..." He gestured toward the window, downward toward the fog-wrapped high school, as if it symbolized everything she would escape. "You're free now, Anna."

Anna nodded slowly. To Arno freedom meant irresponsibility, and to David, kindly detachment. What did freedom mean to her? She would have to learn that too.

"This place where I'm going to live...to keep my home base," David went on. "It's just over the border from Italy, not two hours drive from the village your mother used to talk about. I've seen it, passed through it, many times. I even recognized some of the things she used to tell me about, some of the old things still as they were amidst the new. A hotel was going in when I left. But the place still has a few years to go before they ruin it completely. You can still see it almost as it was before..."

"Oh, no, David, I couldn't go there. It's too soon."

"Too soon?"

"Tell me, are there still little clay cottages, with chickens and goats?"

"A few," said David, "still the same."

157

Anna sighed. "My parents really lived on the dirt floor of one of those places, and smelled the goat and gathered the chicken droppings to trade for milk. And you didn't mention the factory. Is the factory still there?"

David smiled sheepishly. "Larger than ever, creates rather a smog problem."

"No, it's too soon," said Anna. "T.S. Eliot could go back to the village in England, three generations removed from the reasons his parents had to leave. But for me to go back would be almost like saying my parents' struggle was for nothing."

"Pardon me, my dear, but I think that's utter nonsense."

"Maybe. Anyway, it's not for me. I think I'm much too American. I'd be homesick. My parents traveled clear across the Atlantic and then clear across the continent. Maybe the second generation has to rest. Maybe that's why I hate travel. No, I couldn't go with you."

"Not now. But perhaps later you'll change your mind."

"Perhaps."

David got up and sat in the chair again. "But then exactly what are you going to do?"

"Answer all these letters first of all. Since the...what happened, I seem to be developing quite a correspondence. And I'm having dinner next Thursday with Maria, an old...a new friend."

"Yes, my dear, that's fine, but I meant...beyond next week, what are your plans for the future?"

Anna's answer was ready, closer than she had realized. "Maybe I'll write that book. People have been telling me to write a book about teaching, living, in The Mission, the way it was."

"Oh, that sounds like fun!"

"Fun!" Anna laughed. "It'll be damned hard work! As you'd well know if you'd ever written anything but postcards."

David shrugged. "Then why do it? Why not just...enjoy life?" ◖

"Like a tourist? Passing through, tasting here and there?" Anna's voice sounded more snappish than she intended.

David's smile was easy, not hurt but not apologetic either. "It always suited me well enough. As lives go, mine has been...pleasant. Because I'm a...a good tourist. But you..."

"I'm not. Not objective enough. I don't see local color and exotic people. I don't see any point in just...viewing. Why watch how other people live unless we see something to apply to our own lives? Learn it. Live it."

158

David shook his head. "How an Italian could ever turn into such a puritan, I'll never fathom. Everything must be useful to you. A lesson. Teacher. Student. Classroom. The whole world is a classroom, and the lesson for today is...what? I thought when you retired you'd want to be away from all that, but you're incurably the teacher."

Anna laughed. "With only myself left as student."

"Well," said David, "I guess people never change. I suppose we can't change."

"Yes, we can!" Anna surprised even herself by her vehemence. "We can change," she insisted, quietly. "I'm changing."

"How? How are you changing?"

"I..." Anna shrugged. "I don't know."

"The important thing," David said, "is to realize you don't have to live for other people anymore. Don't you see that? It's time to start thinking of yourself."

"Believe me, David," she said slowly, sure, at least, of this one thing, "that's exactly what I'm doing."

David sighed. "I've never really understood you, Anna, though I've admired and loved you. There's always been that...that intensity in you. I've often wondered what it would be like to be in one of your classes. A little frightening, I suspect."

"That's what they tell me," said Anna.

David stood. "And there's nothing more I can do for you."

Anna stood and faced him.

"I'm leaving next week."

Anna nodded, put her arms around his neck and held him tight. As she drew away, he caught both of her hands and pressed them to his lips. Then he quickly turned his head away and began fumbling with the doorknob.

She walked out into the hall with him and watched him go down the stairs. At the foot of the stairs he turned and waved at her. He was smiling again. The lady in overalls closed the front door after him, turned to look upward at Anna and exclaimed, "What a charming man!"

Anna went back into her room. She stood at the window and looked down to the street, watching David walk up the hill to where he had parked the car, in front of her old house. She watched as he glanced up at the house once more, felt with him the last look he took at it before easing himself into his little car. Then the car twirled away

159

from the curb, turning an almost complete circle before plummeting down the hill.

Anna raised her eyes to the wet rooftops, glistening in waves of blinding brightness. The gray sky was whitening to a hard glare. Just to her right, the fog had broken into a streak of blue, as if the sky were about to split wide open and unveil...

"...angel wings!" said Anna, then laughed. She turned and reached for her coat. It was going to be a glorious day for a walk.